CREATORS GONNA
A COLORING BOOK INSPIRED BY THE AWARD WINNING #HASHTAG SERIES

#HOOKUP

Published by: Cambria Hebert

http://www.cambriahebert.com

Interior design by Cover Me Darling

Cover design by Cover Me Darling

Bonus Content Edited by Cassie McCown

Copyright 2017 by Cambria Hebert

Paperback ISBN: 978-1-946836-07-6

#HOOKUP

Your #HookUp for all things #Hashtag.

Missing your favorite #family?

This is your exclusive invitation back into their world.

#HookUp is an explosion of the award-winning #Hashtag series by Cambria Hebert

and makes the perfect collector's item

and addition to the series.

It's a coloring book, but not just any coloring book.

#HookUp includes coloring pages that will rock your world, a #Hashtag-themed word

search, recipes from your favorite characters, and…

Are you ready?

Bonus scenes!

Four bonus scenes total—two of which are brand new!

Find out what your favorite gang is up to these days.

So what are you waiting for?

Get the #HookUp!

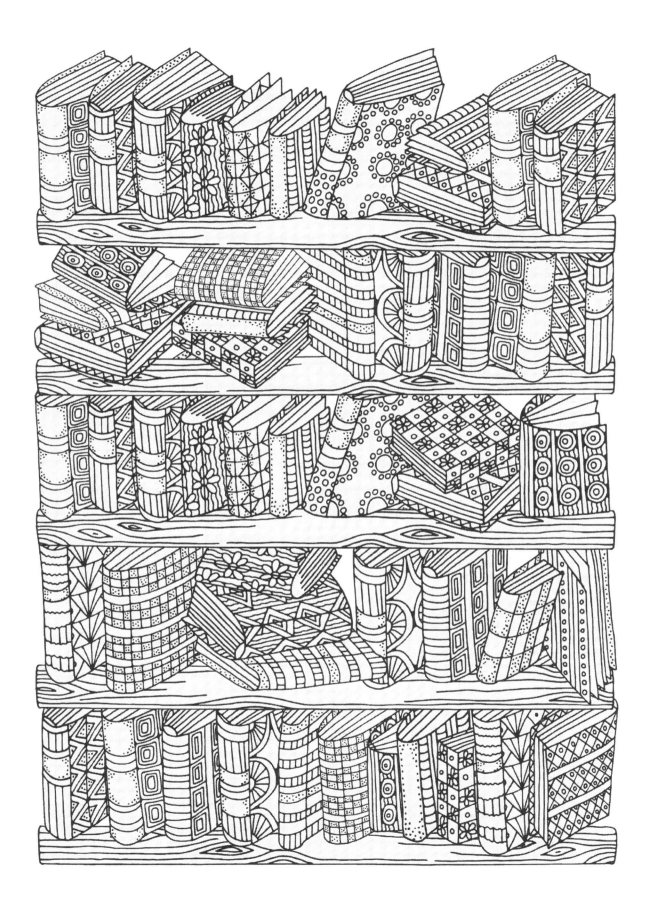

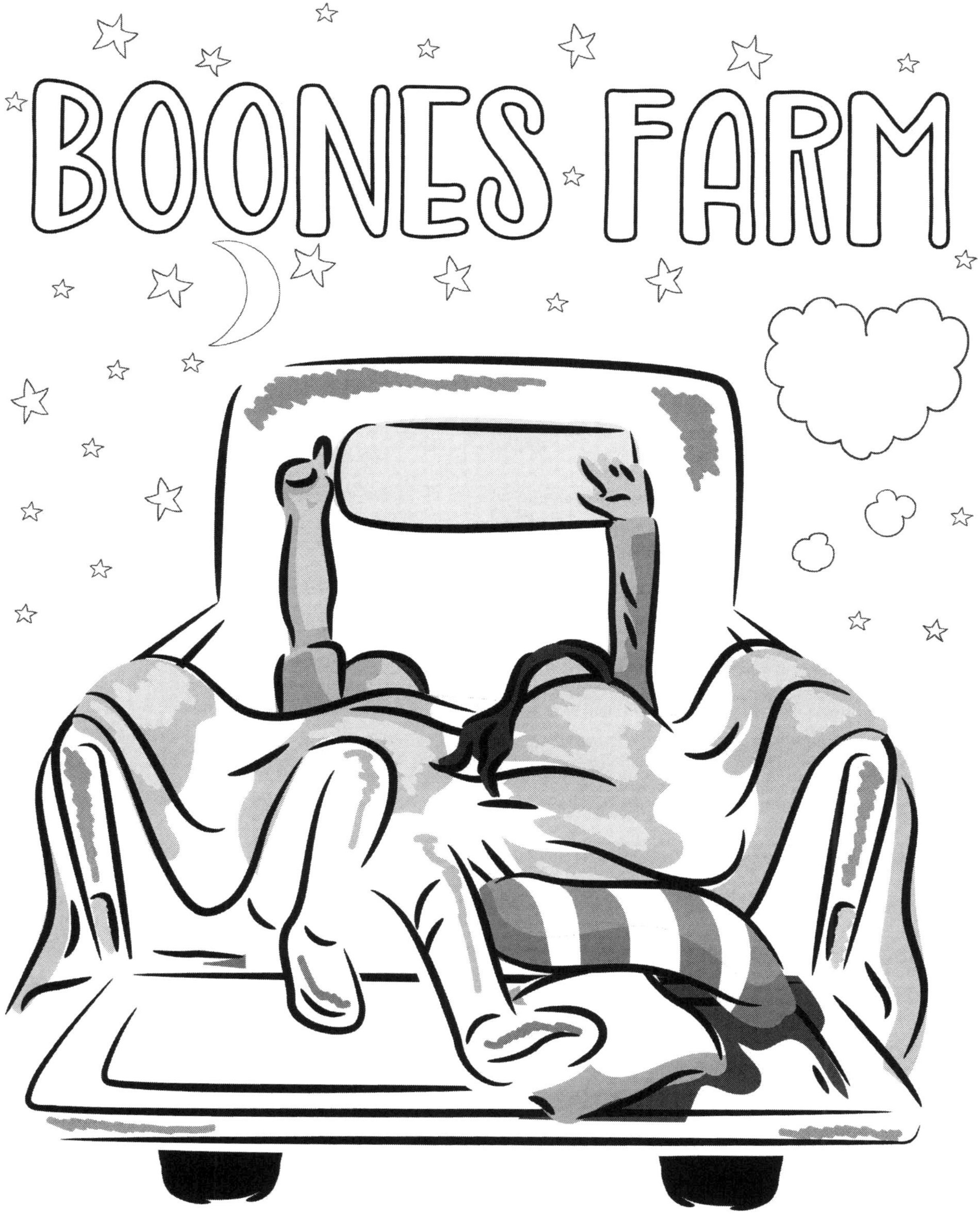
BOONES FARM

BOOKSTORE

LIBRARY →

THERE IS BEAUTY IN IMPERFECTION

MURPHY

#NEWSFLASH
ROMEO AND JULIET IS SOOO LAST CENTURY
NOW IT'S ROMEO AND RIMMEL
♥

...ALPHABUZZFEED

#NERD IS THE NEW SEXY

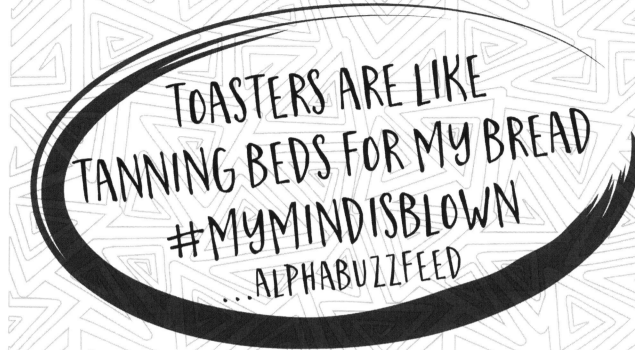

#HASHTAG NEXT GENERATION

#HASHTAG WORD SEARCH

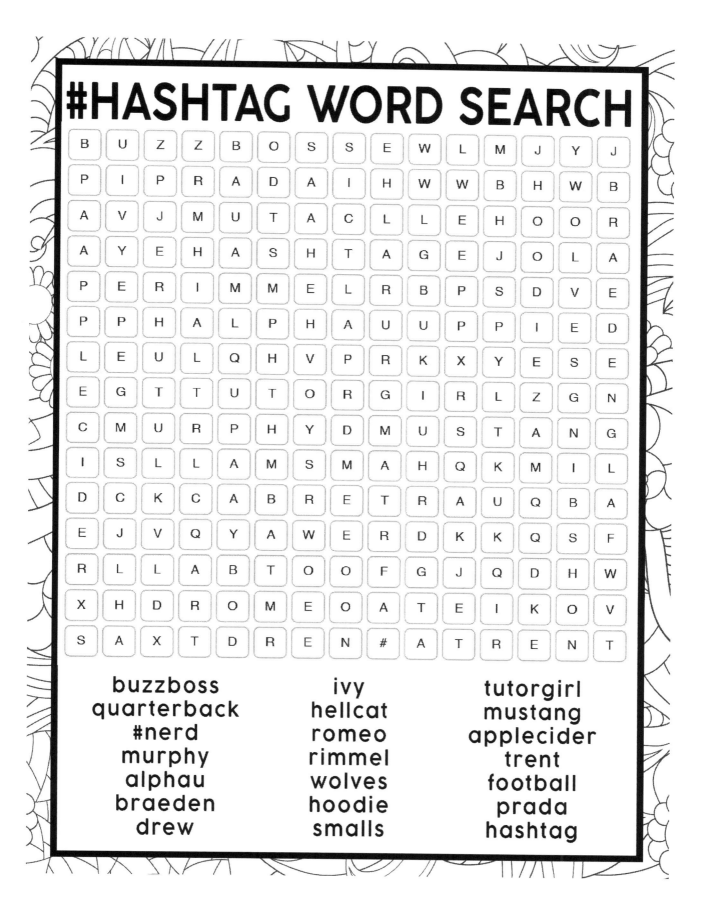

B	U	Z	Z	B	O	S	S	E	W	L	M	J	Y	J
P	I	P	R	A	D	A	I	H	W	W	B	H	W	B
A	V	J	M	U	T	A	C	L	L	E	H	O	O	R
A	Y	E	H	A	S	H	T	A	G	E	J	O	L	A
P	E	R	I	M	M	E	L	R	B	P	S	D	V	E
P	P	H	A	L	P	H	A	U	U	P	P	I	E	D
L	E	U	L	Q	H	V	P	R	K	X	Y	E	S	E
E	G	T	T	U	T	O	R	G	I	R	L	Z	G	N
C	M	U	R	P	H	Y	D	M	U	S	T	A	N	G
I	S	L	L	A	M	S	M	A	H	Q	K	M	I	L
D	C	K	C	A	B	R	E	T	R	A	U	Q	B	A
E	J	V	Q	Y	A	W	E	R	D	K	K	Q	S	F
R	L	L	A	B	T	O	O	F	G	J	Q	D	H	W
X	H	D	R	O	M	E	O	A	T	E	I	K	O	V
S	A	X	T	D	R	E	N	#	A	T	R	E	N	T

buzzboss	ivy	tutorgirl
quarterback	hellcat	mustang
#nerd	romeo	applecider
murphy	rimmel	trent
alphau	wolves	football
braeden	hoodie	prada
drew	smalls	hashtag

#WHERESROMEO

#HOOKUP WORD SCRAMBLE

RMAYNALD TGHKINS

☐☐☐☐☐☐☐☐ ☐☐☐☐☐☐☐

ERFBEO ENOANY SEEL

☐☐☐☐☐☐ ☐☐☐☐☐☐☐ ☐☐☐☐

DOHOWTUCN

☐☐☐☐☐☐☐☐☐

#OWERELTV

☐☐☐☐☐☐☐☐

IFRES OEEBFR GSUY

☐☐☐☐☐ ☐☐☐☐☐☐ ☐☐☐☐

HLESL YAHE

☐☐☐☐☐ ☐☐☐☐

RATF RTAYP

☐☐☐☐☐ ☐☐☐☐☐

(COLOR, CUT OUT, LAMINATE!)

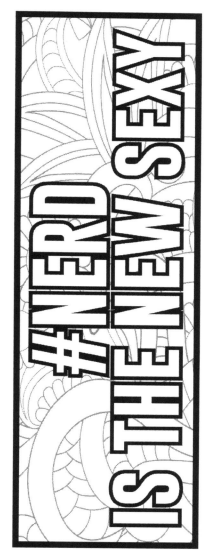

#NERD IS THE NEW NEW SEXY

OFFICIAL #HOOKUP BOOKMARKS

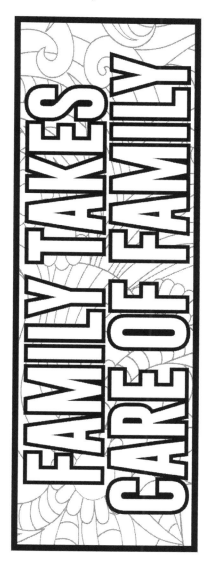

FAMILY TAKES CARE OF FAMILY

#HOOKUP

#NERD
SLOW COOKER APPLE CIDER

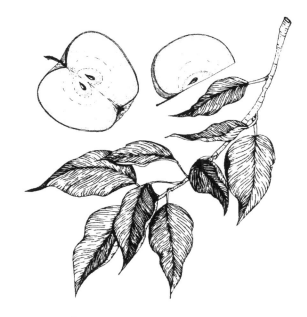

ingredients:

1 bottle of apple cider (64oz)

3 cinnamon sticks

1 tsp whole allspice

1 tsp whole cloves

1/3 cup brown sugar

Directions :

Combine cider, cinnamon sticks and sugar in slow cooker. Wrap cloves and allspice in cheesecloth and place inside. Bring to a boil then reduce heat and simmer on low for one hour.

Garnish with cinnamon sticks & whipped cream!

RIMMEL APPROVED!

SMURF BALLS

THE OFFICIAL SHOT OF ALPHA U

ingredients:

1 ounce Blue Curacao
1 ounce Coconut Rum
1 ounce Sweet & Sour
Blue Skittles

Directions :

Pour all liquid into shaker filled

with ice.

Shake well.

Pour into shot glass.

Drop 2 blue skittles into shot.

CAUTION!
WILL MAKE YOUR
TONGUE BLUE

DRINK UP!

*makes one shot

*Drink Responsibly

BRAEDEN'S BROWNIES

DON'T FORGET THE SPRINKLES!

Ingredients:

1 1/2 sticks butter
2 eggs
1 cup sugar
2/3 cup packed brown sugar
2 tsp. vanilla extract
3/4 cup flour
3/4 cocoa powder
pinch of salt

Fudge-y Topping:

1 cup semi-sweet chocolate chips
1/2 cup milk chocolate chips
1/2 cup heavy cream
SPRINKLES!

Directions:

Preheat oven to 350 degrees.
Melt butter in the microwave.
Whisk in sugars, eggs, milk, salt, and vanilla. Then whisk in cocoa powder, mix until smooth.
Add flour slowly, until combined.
Spread in 9x9 greased pan.
Bake for 25-30 minutes or until a toothpick inserted comes out clean. Cool.
Heat heavy cream in a medium sauce pan. Add chocolate chips. Stir occasionally until smooth.
Pour topping over brownies
Add LOTS of sprinkles.
Then add some more.
Refridgerate until fudge-y topping is set.

HASHTAG SERIES BONUS SCENE #1

STARRING RIMMEL & IVY

BY CAMBRIA HEBERT

This scene takes place the day Rimmel and Ivy
first meet as roommates at the dorm at Alpha U.
*previously published in the #Nerd hardback edition

RIMMEL

I WAS ALREADY COLD.

Not even fifteen minutes after my flight from Florida landed here in Maryland and I was already asking myself why I chose a college up north when I was used to living in the South.

It wasn't quite September, but it already felt like autumn here. The second I stepped out onto the sidewalk to hopefully flag down a cab, I noticed. The air here was cooler, the breeze not as gentle. And the humidity?

There wasn't any.

Not that I'd really miss the humidity.

At least without it, my hair would be a little easier to manage.

Like you even managed it before, a snarky voice in the back of my head reminded me. I snorted, and the man walking in front of me jerked and spun around like something was after him.

My cheeks heated and I looked down at the sidewalk.

The line for the cabs was long. As usual. So I waited toward the back of the crowd until most everyone had found a car. But eventually, I had to move up and wave my hand out to one so they would stop.

The first two times, the cab drivers kept going.

I swear I could hear them laughing as they passed.

"Stupid cabbies," I muttered.

As another one came over the small hill toward me, I was determined to flag him down. Standing out here half the day was not my idea of a good time. I needed to unpack and then get to the bookstore. I didn't want to end up with the crappy leftover picks of used textbooks.

I stretched out my arm as far as I could and pushed back the sleeve of the too-big, brown sweater I was wearing so I could use my hand.

The cab driver looked at me; our eyes met through the windshield. I knew that look. He was going to pass me, too.

What was it about me that was so . . . so . . . easy to look over?

That's the way you wanted it, the voice in my head piped up again.

Stupid voice.

Even if it was right.

I didn't give up, though. Determination had me stretching my hand out just a little bit farther. My money was just as good as the next person's.

Behind me, a loud whistle cut through the air, and I jerked and stumbled backward. I gasped and pressed a hand to my chest. My goodness!

The cab driver who'd just started driving past slammed on his brakes and stopped at the curb just ahead of me.

I grumbled to myself as I strong-armed my giant suitcase back up onto its wheels. I'd knocked the stupid thing over when I fell back. I don't know how. It practically weighed more than me.

A rich laugh floated over my head, and I looked up, pushing back the mop of dark hair hanging in my face.

"Not your day, is it?" a man said to me.

I looked around as if searching for the person he was talking to.

His white teeth flashed, and he motioned at me with his chin. "Need a hand with that?"

He was talking to me.

I fought the urge to shrink back. Hadn't I just been standing here wishing I wasn't so unnoticeable? Now that someone actually saw me, my reaction was to hide.

I was a hot mess.

The guy, who seemed to maybe be a year or two older than me, had dark hair and dark eyes. He was taller than me, but that really wasn't an accomplishment because everyone was, and he looked like he hadn't shaved in a while.

He was actually kind of good-looking. If a girl liked that sort of rumpled style.

I had no idea what kind of "style" I liked when it came to men. I never bothered to ask myself. Still, as I stood here looking at him smiling, I realized he wasn't it. There was something missing from this guy, something I wasn't even sure about.

He cleared his throat, and I realized he'd asked me a question.

Good Lord, I'm standing here like a weirdo, gaping at him!

"No thanks," I finally replied, trying to keep my voice from squeaking. "I can handle it."

His eyes crinkled at the corners and he laughed. "Sweetheart, I hate to break it to you, but that suitcase is the one handling you."

I recoiled from his flirtatious tone. I didn't flirt with men. I wasn't interested in them.

Well, I guess technically I was because I was heterosexual, but I wasn't interested in dating.

He laughed as I continued to stand there having a mental showdown with myself and came forward. "Having trouble getting a cab?"

"Yeah," I said. No point in lying. He likely saw me being passed up.

"Take mine," he said. "I'll whistle down another one."

"Is that the secret?" I wondered. "Whistling really loud?"

He chuckled and picked up my bag before I could stop him. "Doesn't hurt."

The cab driver got out of his seat and came around to open the trunk. The stranger put my suitcase inside.

"What do you have in there?" he drawled once it was in. "A hundred pairs of shoes?"

Yeah, 'cause I looked like a girl with a hundred pairs of shoes. "Books," I replied.

"Ah, a woman with a sexy mind."

Ew.

How dare he think about my mind that way! Not that I should be surprised. That's all men ever thought about.

Sex.

"Well, thanks for the cab," I said and started forward, skirting around him so we didn't get too close.

He opened the door of the cab and held it for me. "Anytime."

Inside, I leaned forward and said, "Alpha University dorms."

When I sat back, the stranger was still holding open the door and looking at me. It made me uncomfortable and slightly embarrassed.

"So what's your name, girl with the sexy mind?"

"I don't have one," I said, my voice high pitched. Then I shot forward, grabbed the door, and slammed it closed.

The shock on the guy's face was almost funny.

The cabbie laughed and pulled away from the corner.

"Guess you weren't interested," he drawled.

"No," I said, then turned my face to stare out the window.

I most certainly wasn't interested in guys who tried to pick me up at the airport. I wasn't interested in dating at all.

There wasn't one guy in this entire state that could change my mind on that fact.

I wasn't here at Alpha U to date. I was here to study.

#

IVy

BY THE TIME I MADE it to the second floor with every last bag, box, and suitcase I brought to campus with me, I was certain I'd completed my yearly quota for cardio.

It made me regret not taking my brother up on his offer to drive behind me and help me get settled in.

'Course, if I'd agreed to that, Drew would have spent the entire time bossing me around. Then he would've given me a lecture about the reasons I didn't need so many clothes.

As if there were any kind of logical argument for that.

Besides, I was a big girl. A sophomore in college. I could handle move-in day all on my own. I thought about last year, my freshman year, when I first showed up here at the dorm. Both my parents and my brothers were with me.

We looked like a herd of cattle moving across the campus. Even though it was embarrassing as hell, I'd still been grateful because I'd been so nervous. It was the first time I'd really been "on my own" without family hovering around me.

I had no idea what to expect.

It didn't take long to figure out what everyone else expected. I was blond, blue-eyed, and liked clothes and makeup. That instantly gave people an impression. So naturally, I believed what everyone else thought, what everyone else assumed.

It was fun to be the party girl. It was fun to be the one who got invited to everything. Parties I could actually go to because I didn't have my annoying brothers following me around or my mom calling me every ten minutes to remind me of my curfew.

After I dumped everything in the center of my assigned room, I looked around the small rectangle, deciding on which side I should take. My roommate wasn't here yet, so that meant I got first dibs on the beds.

Not like it was some big advantage, though. They were the exact same, just on opposite sides of the room.

I decided on the one to my left, for no other reason than that's the side I naturally gravitated toward. Using my feet, I pushed all my stuff over to that side of the room and then set the box with all my new bedding on the end of the mattress. It was all freshly washed and ready to be put on.

Laughter floated into the empty room from out in the hall and distracted me. I pulled out my phone and texted my friend Missy to see if she was back on campus yet. We'd met freshman year and had become friends pretty quickly.

Missy was here and was on the floor below mine. I abandoned my stuff and went down to her room.

The door was propped open as her roommate moved in a few boxes. Missy's stuff was already inside, and she was unpacking a bunch of yellow and gray bedding.

"Hey, girl!" she chirped. "How was your summer?"

"It was good. How about you?"

"Same," she replied, tossing some pillows on the bed. "So guess who knows of a really good party tonight?"

"You've been on campus, what, like twenty minutes, and already you have the down low on a party? Where do you get your info?"

Missy giggled. "I have my ways."

"Mm-hmm," I said and started looking through a box of her clothes. She had some cute stuff in there.

She sighed. "Fine. I heard some cheerleaders talking about it out in the hallway."

I laughed. "So where is this party?"

"Out in the field."

I'd been to lots of parties out there last year. They were fun, and it was a popular place for the football players to party. So basically, that's where the in crowd went.

"Sounds good to me."

"Awesome! We need to let off some steam before the semester starts."

"Wear this," I said and tossed her a black lacey top.

She snatched it up and laid it out on her bed. "Now I just have to search for the pants that match."

"Speaking of, I better go unpack or I'm not gonna be able to find anything to wear either."

Missy waved her fingers at me and reached for another box. "I'll come get you later and we can go to the party together."

I told her my room number and left, taking myself back up the stairs to unpack. When I arrived back on the second floor and stepped out of the stairwell into the hall, I noticed there was crap lying everywhere.

Like it looked like some kind of stuff-nado ripped through and left the place littered with random crap. Pens, pencils, little notebooks, lip balm, gum . . .

A couple girls walking down the hall snickered, looking in the direction of my room.

I hurried down the hall, noticing the door to my room was open. The loud sound of things being dropped or spilled echoed out.

I picked my way carefully over all the stuff as someone came rushing out the door and almost barreled into me.

"Whoa!" I said and backed up, my foot snapping a pencil in half.

"I'm sorry!" a girl said in a soft yet somehow squeaky voice. Then she dropped onto the floor and began picking up everything.

"Is this your dorm room?" I asked, staring down at the top of her dark head.

"Yes."

"Oh, awesome. I'm Ivy. Your roomie."

The girl's head snapped up and her eyes widened. She had on large, black-rimmed glasses and no makeup at all. Even though most of her wild hair covered half her face, I knew she was pretty. Well, if she combed her hair and maybe put on some lip-gloss.

She stood up with stuff filling her hands and smiled at me kind of shyly. "I'm not usually this messy. My bag spilled when I was trying to find the room key."

"No worries," I said and bent to pick up everything else. "If you have as much stuff as I do, then I don't blame you for dropping half of it. Those stairs are a workout."

She turned and went back in the room, and I followed, letting the door close behind us. I dropped my handful of her things on the end of her bed, and she did the same.

"I'm Rimmel," she said, pushing her hair back over her shoulders.

"Like the makeup," I said.

"What?"

I gave her a bewildered look. "There's a makeup brand called Rimmel London. Haven't you heard of it?"

"I don't wear makeup," she said, shy, and ducked her head.

"Well, you're pretty enough without it," I answered.

She glanced up and smiled. Something told me this girl was the shiest person I'd ever meet. I knew just by looking at her she didn't have very much confidence. I guess I understood her in that regard. I just handled my lack of it a lot different than her. For me, I tried too hard to get people to like me and I worried a lot about what other people thought. But Rimmel? I knew from just two minutes in her presence that she was the kind who didn't try at all.

And where was all her stuff? She literally had one huge suitcase and a bag. Where the hell were all her clothes?

Speaking of . . . She was wearing an unfortunate brown sweater that looked like it came from the nineteen thirties and a pair of loose, dark-colored pants that probably had a drawstring waist.

She needed a fashion intervention. STAT.

She was standing there looking at me like she was either:

A) Waiting for me to say something rude to her.

Or

B) Trying to come up with something to say to start a conversation.

Both reasons made me feel kinda bad. Like it bothered me she expected people to be rude to her. 'Course, I totally saw why she would think that way. People were mean; women were vicious to other women.

Hence, I did myself up every day and partied with the right crowd.

Rimmel was small, socially awkward, and judging by the mess in the hall, she was clumsy. She'd probably been bullied half her life.

"So," I said conversationally, going over to my side of the room. "I picked this bed, but if you'd rather have it, I'm happy to trade."

"This side of the room is fine, thanks," she said and wrestled her giant suitcase onto its side so she could unzip it.

"Did you go here last year?" I asked.

"Yeah, but I was in a different dorm."

"Cool. I was in this dorm last year, too. I was on the first floor, though. Let me tell you . . . Made moving in a lot easier. I have a couple friends in the building. Missy's going to stop by later. We're going to a party on campus. You should come."

I was met with an odd kind of silence, so I looked away from the bedding I was stretching onto my mattress and turned to her.

She was staring at me with shock in her eyes. "You're inviting me to a party?"

I shrugged. "Sure. You don't like parties?"

"No."

Oh boy. I hoped she wasn't going to be the kind of roommate that went running to the floor advisor when I was late for curfew.

"Parties aren't my thing," she said by way of explanation.

"Do you care if parties are my thing?" I asked.

She shook her head. "Is bringing random guys back to our room your thing?"

"Not at all." I assured her.

"I don't care if you like parties." She shrugged.

"Whew." I blew out a breath. "For a minute there I thought you were going to be a pain in my ass."

Rimmel's eyes widened.

"Kidding," I said and laughed. She took everything so seriously. I glanced at her suitcase. It was filled with books.

"I have lots of clothes. If you ever want to borrow anything, feel free."

"Thanks," she mumbled. "Feel free to use some of the drawer space over here."

"Really? That's awesome of you."

She turned back to her books and started unpacking them all, placing them on the shelves above the desk beside her bed.

She didn't seem bad for a roommate. I could have been assigned one that was much worse. But she definitely didn't seem like the type that was going to be a fast friend.

I kinda wondered if she would ever be a friend at all.

#

RIMMEL

SHE WAS A TALKER. BUBBLY, sunny, and all-around chatty.

We were complete opposites. But she did seem nice, definitely not judgmental or stuck-up like a lot of the girls I'd met.

She even told me I was pretty, which was arguably the nicest thing anyone had said to me on this campus so far. Aside from my previous professors of course.

It worried me that she liked to party and was probably part of the "in" crowd. Of course, that might have been a good thing. She probably wouldn't spend much time in the room because of her social life, so I would have it to myself a lot.

And my goodness did the girl have a ton of clothes. It was like a freaking department store on her side of the room. She had so much she used some of my drawers on my side.

Not that I cared. I barely had any at all.

"Hey," Ivy said after a remarkably long silence, not talking about campus, classes, the food court, the party tonight, and literally everything else that popped into her head. "I'm gonna go grab some bottled water and a few things for the mini fridge. Wanna come?"

"You have a car?"

She nodded. "Yeah. If you ever need a ride anywhere, let me know."

"Thanks," I said. She really was being nice. "But no, I'm going to head over to the bookstore. I can give you some money for the supplies, though. Go half with you."

"Nah." She waved me off. "I got it this time. You can come with next time and help pay."

"Okay."

She was on her phone, her fingers flying over it rapidly. A few moments later, it made a sound like she got a text.

"I'm meeting Missy downstairs. She needs stuff, too. I'll introduce you later."

When she was gone, I sat on the bed with an exhale. I didn't have any friends. I had no idea how to even make one. It was easier for me to connect to animals. Animals just seemed so much simpler to understand.

I finished unpacking completely and went and bought all my books before Ivy came back. Once everything she'd bought was put away, she started riffling through all her clothes to find something to wear to the party.

I thought she looked good in the skinny jeans and loose-fitting top, but when I said that, she laughed and said it wasn't party clothes.

A short while later, there was a knock on our door. I looked up from the book I was reading—well, trying to read (did I mention she liked to talk?)—and watched Ivy bounce over and open up the door.

"Heeyyy," she sang. Her shiny blond hair was long and bounced around when she moved. Ivy was really pretty. She had a nice womanly shape (as opposed to my boy-like one), manageable hair the color of sun, and wide blue eyes that saw without the aid of glasses.

She was dressed in a pair of skintight dark-wash jeans with rips in the knees, dark-brown boots with wedge heels, and a low-cut navy-blue blouse with an embroidered white design around the hem.

"Hey," an unfamiliar voice replied. "I love those jeans."

"Thanks. They're new."

The girls came into the room, and I glanced behind Ivy at who I assumed was her friend Missy. She was gorgeous. Like she could be in magazines. Her long, dark hair was sleek and shiny, her features balanced, and her skin was so smooth it almost looked unreal. She was thin and graceful, not too short, but not really too tall either. And her eyes were a beautiful shade of gray.

"Missy, this is my roommate Rimmel." Ivy began. "Rimmel, this is Missy."

"Hi," I said, giving her a small wave and mustering up a smile I hoped didn't look awkward.

"Hey," she replied. Her voice was friendly, and she smiled, but almost as soon as she looked at me, I saw the assessment in her gaze before she looked away.

It was the same look I'd been given a thousand times before. The same reason I didn't bother making friends. It made me feel like I'd been given a test I hadn't studied for and therefore failed. Ivy turned away to grab her cell phone and slide a few things in the back pocket of her jeans.

"I really like your bedspread," Missy told me with genuine kindness in her tone.

"Thanks," I said, then wondered if perhaps I'd just been too fast in assuming she didn't like me.

"You comin' with tonight?"

I shook my head. "No. Parties aren't really my thing."

"I told her to come!" Ivy piped in.

"Maybe next time?" Missy asked.

"Maybe," I echoed, even though I knew I'd never.

"Okay, well, we're going. Don't wait up!" Ivy wiggled her fingers at me, and I smiled.

When she was gone, I looked over at her side of the room at all her colorful clothes and decorations. As far as roommates went, I guessed I could do a lot worse.

# # #

IVY

TECHNICALLY, THE SEMESTER HADN'T STARTED yet, but the big open field where everyone partied was full of people. I wouldn't be surprised if people came back early just so they could party.

I parked on the edge of the dirt road beside some tall grass, and we walked over to where everyone had gathered. There was no big bonfire tonight like there usually was during football season. It was a little early for that.

But some of the guys here had their trucks pulled up close to the clearing and their headlights were on, illuminating the darkness.

Someone had loud music pumping through their speakers, and people were dancing, laughing, and drinking all over the place.

Missy and I found the drinks, helped ourselves, and then went around mingling with some of the familiar faces and checking out the new ones.

On the other side of the field was a large group of guys, all huge and all loud. I knew immediately it was the Wolves. Alpha University was serious about their football, and those players were like celebrities around campus.

My eyes scanned the group for one player in particular, the quarterback, Romeo. He was basically the alpha of the pack. He was tall, blond, and had a set of blue eyes that made every single girl on campus swoon.

To say he was popular would be an understatement.

He was the king of the status pyramid. If you were in with Romeo, then you were in with everyone. Period.

Maybe that's why I sought him out. That kind of power was attractive, but it was also noteworthy. Watching to see what he was up to was just natural curiosity.

He was easy to spot. His blond hair was like a beacon against the dark night. Of course, people surrounded him, and he laughed at whatever the dude beside him was saying. Romeo was also a big player. There wasn't a girl on campus who'd managed to hold his attention for more than a few days.

Honestly, I never tried. I'd thought about it. Like I said, being in with him would basically make sure I was in with everyone. But something held me back. Maybe it was because I knew Romeo wasn't the guy for me.

Or maybe it was because I hadn't had enough to drink yet.

As I sipped at the beer in my hand, my eyes slid to Braeden, Romeo's partner in crime. Those two were always together, completely attached at the hip. It was kinda adorable.

Every party one was at last year, the other one was, too. I guess the same could be said about Missy and me, but my friendship with her was only a year old. The one between Romeo and Braeden was clearly a lot more cemented than that.

Braeden was a dog. Worse than Romeo. He was forever cracking some kind of lame joke, and he hit on everything with boobs that walked by.

He was good-looking, though. I'd never admit it out loud, but he was more my type than Romeo. I liked Braeden's dark looks. His dark hair and eyes gave him a little more of a brooding quality. But when he smiled—which he did a lot because the guy thought he was hilarious—it transformed that brooding air into an ornery troublemaker.

I'd never admit this out loud either, but he was kinda charming.

"He's so hot." Missy sighed.

I followed her gaze back to the same place I was looking. "Romeo?" I asked.

"Yeah, him, too."

I glanced at her, and we both laughed.

"Come on," she said. "Let's go dance."

I downed the rest of my beer on the way to the dance floor, and I lost myself in the music and fun. Guys came and went. I danced with a lot of them. One even stole a kiss before I laughed and pulled away.

Hours passed, and the beer flowed. My feet were hurting from all the fun when I finally announced I was ready to go.

Missy drove my car back to the dorm. She was the DD tonight, because after just two drinks, it became clear that a summer without drinking at all had lowered my tolerance.

When I finally let myself in the dorm, it was after two a.m. I'd forgotten I had stuff still piled on my side of the room, and I tripped over it and hit my knee on the bed.

"Oww!" I howled.

A startled, muffled yell came from the other side of the room, and a small light clicked on.

I giggled when Rimmel blinked at me. Her hair was wild. "Sorry, Rimmel. I forgot about all this stuff."

"Are you just getting in?" she asked, squinting at the clock beside her bed, trying to read it without her glasses.

"Yeah." I laughed. I knew I was still buzzed, but I couldn't keep from acting like it. "You missed a good party."

"Are you drunk?" she asked.

"Who me?" I pointed to myself. "Nah."

Rimmel giggled and pointed at my bed. "Better lie down before you hurt yourself."

"Good idea," I said and dropped on the bed.

"Might want to take off those heels."

"My feet do hurt," I said, and I started to pull them off. It took forever and I almost gave up.

Finally, when they were gone, I quickly exchanged my clothes for a set of super cute pink pajamas and used a wipe to remove all my makeup. Sleeping in makeup was a big skin no-no. I might have been tipsy, but I wasn't so drunk I would neglect my skin care.

"Ivy?" Rimmel asked from somewhere in the pile of blankets on her bed.

"Yeah?"

"Did you drive tonight?"

"Missy drove us back. She was the DD."

"Oh, that's good. I'm glad."

I finished up and poured myself into bed and sighed.

Rimmel reached up and turned off the light, the room sinking into blissful darkness.

"I better not be hung-over tomorrow," I muttered.

Rimmel's laugh floated over to my side.

A few minutes later, Rimmel's voice filled the darkness. I was surprised she was talking to me again. She was usually pretty quiet. "Ivy, if you ever go to a party and need a ride home, you can call me. I don't have a car, but I'll figure something out."

"You'd do that?"

"Sure."

"Wow. You're a good friend," I said and snuggled down into the pillows.

Rimmel didn't say anything at all.

When I was drifting off to sleep, I thought I heard her speak again, but maybe it was the beer.

"This is definitely going to be an interesting year," she whispered.

My last thought before falling asleep was, I agree.

HASHTAG SERIES BONUS SCENE #2

STARRING ROMEO AND RIMMEL

BY CAMBRIA HEBERT

This scene takes place right before the start of #Poser (Hashtag book #5)
previously published in the #Nerd hardback edition

ROMEO

"I'LL TAKE IT." I WAS standing on the freshly manicured lawn, staring up at the two-story, four-bedroom house.

It was a nice place. Actually, it was better than nice. It was in one of the best neighborhoods in this town and, despite being an older home, was newly redone.

I wasn't about to rent anything less than this for the most important person in my life to live in.

Beside me, the real estate agent tried to hide her excitement. "That's wonderful, Mr. Anderson. I'm so thrilled I could help you find something so quickly."

I turned toward her and gave her my full smile. "You're good at your job."

In reality, I knew exactly what I wanted and had said as much before I even got in her car. I was working against a ticking clock. I didn't have time to tour half the town.

The first place she showed me was in the wrong neighborhood, and it didn't have an alarm system.

The second place didn't have a garage.

When we got in the car again, I told her to take me to the Palisades and show me something worth my time.

"But the price . . ." she said, like Rimmel's safety, my entire family's safety, could have a price tag on it.

She didn't even finish the sentence because the look on my face said it all.

I might be good-looking and laidback, but I knew how to convey what I wanted with a single glance.

She cleared her throat and drove straight here.

The second I walked through the wide yellow front door, saw the dark hardwood floors, light-painted walls, open concept, and spacious bedrooms, I knew I'd found the one.

It also helped that it had a fenced-in backyard, a garage, and a new security system. I could almost picture Murphy perched on the black granite island, waiting for a barefooted Rim to hand him a pile of treats.

Beside me, the real estate agent blushed under the effects of my praise.

Nah. It was my smile that had her all flustered.

"Now we can set an appointment to go over the application, sign the papers, and of course, the first and last month will be due," she rushed out.

I lifted my hand and cut her off. "I'm ready to sign now. I'll go back to your office with you."

"But I'll need to call the homeowner and—"

Again, I held up my hand. "Of course," I replied smoothly. "I'll get on the line and introduce myself, let him know I need to get this done quickly, as I'll be leaving for camp for the Knights."

She nodded with wide eyes. I gave her another smile, and she practically giggled.

"I'm sure once he hears I'll cut him a check for the first year's rent, in full, this afternoon, he will accommodate the quick timeline."

"The full year . . ." Her voice trailed.

I smiled even wider.

A few hours later, all the papers were signed, the rent was taken care of, and the homeowner authorized me to take possession of the property immediately.

And that's how you get shit done.

Well, maybe not you.

But that's how I did.

I walked out of the office feeling pretty damn pleased with myself. When I climbed in the Hellcat and fired up the engine, I tossed the paperwork on the empty seat beside me and thought about how to tell Rim.

When I'd told her I had stuff to do today, I knew she would never have guessed I'd be going out house hunting.

A little of the confidence I felt wavered.

She wasn't going to like this.

Not at first anyway.

I found it cute as hell and sort of charming that Rim wasn't affected by my charisma and megawatt smile like everyone else . . . except, of course, when I needed to get what I wanted.

Convincing her to move in with me on a permanent basis was an occasion I coulda used some of my manly goods for coercion.

But it wasn't going to be easy.

I smiled and threw the Cat into reverse.

That's okay. I liked a challenge.

#

RIMMEL

ROMEO WAS UP TO SOMETHING.

I knew it as sure as I knew my own name.

I was standing in the small storage room at the shelter, taking stock of supplies, when I felt his familiar body conform to mine.

His clean scent enveloped me as his arms wound around my waist, and I melted farther against him, surrendering all my weight.

A low sound filled the enclosed space as his lips gently sucked my earlobe into his mouth. His teeth pulled gently and then released to press moist, soft kisses in the same spot.

Goose bumps broke out all over my body as he nuzzled into my neck, bending so his body hunched around mine, completely overtaking me.

With a heavy sigh, my head fell to the side, granting him all the access he needed to continue teasing my flesh in the most seductive way.

"Come here often?" he purred against my ear, and I shivered when his hot breath tickled the flesh he'd already teased.

I wanted to laugh, but it came out more of a groan. "I will if this is what happens when I do."

His deep chuckle vibrated against my back. I lifted one arm and curved it around his neck, letting my fingers play in the ends of his hair. Keeping my back against his front, I looked up so he could cover my mouth with his.

The angle of our bodies and faces should have made the kiss difficult.

But I'd never had a kiss that was anything less than bliss with Romeo.

Our bodies fit together perfectly. It didn't matter where we stood or how awkward the position. His tongue slid out almost instantly and brushed against my upper lip. I opened for him, and it delved farther in, coaxing mine out to play.

My fingers tightened against the back of his neck and I pulled him down farther. We kissed for long moments more, barely surfacing for air before he pulled back enough to lick across my lips one final time.

"Hey, baby," Romeo greeted, a lopsided smirk curving the lips I was just devouring.

"Hi."

He lowered his head to kiss me again.

"You finished all your stuff?" I asked after our lips touched. What stuff he was out doing all morning I didn't know. He was being all secretive like.

Hence, I knew he was up to something.

"Yep."

My eyes narrowed when he offered nothing further, and it made him laugh. He knew I was dying to know what it was he'd been doing.

"You finished here?" he asked, glancing at the shelves.

"Sure," I said and closed up the small room once we stepped out. I could finish this later. He was leaving soon for training camp, and every time I thought about it, a pang of homesickness hit me.

He wasn't even gone, and I was already homesick for him.

I know. It didn't make much sense to be homesick for a person. The very definition of the word was to feel a longing for your home.

Well, my home wasn't a place.

It was a person, this person.

"I got something I wanna show you," he said, entwining our fingers and pulling me toward the front door.

I called out a hasty good-bye to Michelle and barely had time to grab my bag off the counter as he practically dragged me outside.

"My legs don't go as fast as yours," I reminded him.

Every step for him was like two for me.

Geesh, he was excited.

"Smalls." He sighed. "Why ya gotta be so slow?"

Before I could tell him how rude I thought he was, he scooped me up and tossed me over his shoulder. I squealed and hung on to my glasses so they wouldn't fall off my face. "Romeo!"

"I don't have all day, baby," he said, settling his large palm over my butt. "We got somewhere to be."

When we got to his car, he stopped and opened the door.

"My car is here," I reminded him.

"Hunk of junk," he muttered.

I hit him on the butt. "I heard that!"

He swung me back over his shoulder and, in one sweeping movement, planted me in the passenger seat of his car. After he leaned down and buckled me in, he pulled back, crouching in the open door so we were almost at eye level.

His bright-blue gaze swept over my face and his entire appearance softened. Lightly, he caressed my cheek with the backs of his knuckles. "You're really fucking beautiful."

I echoed his movements, skimming my fingers over his cheek. "So are you."

"I have a request," he said.

See? He totally was hatching some plan.

"And what would that be?" I mused, falling prey to the way his eyes made me feel like the only girl in the entire world.

"Don't yell at me."

I scowled as he stood up. "Roman Anderson, what did you do?"

He shut the door on my demand, and I watched him cross in front of the hood on his way to the driver's side. The way he moved almost made me forget I was supposed to be badgering him for answers.

The way he moved was almost as intoxicating as his kisses.

So fluid and at ease. He was so comfortable in his skin it showed in every move he made. Some men had to force the air of confidence around them. Some felt the need to overcompensate for whatever they thought they lacked.

Not Romeo.

He just was.

We held hands as he drove. Occasionally, he would have to wrap both our hands around the stick shift so he could change gears. I didn't bother asking him again what he'd done that would make me yell, because in truth, I didn't want to yell at Romeo.

I wanted to hold his hand in the silence that wasn't really silent. I wanted to be with him in this moment and commit it to my memory to pull out when he was away and I was feeling empty without him.

You see, even when we didn't speak, I could still hear him. He loved me so deep that words became secondary to the way he made me feel every single day.

He turned into a neighborhood I'd never been in before, and my eyes immediately went out the window, captured by the beauty.

I felt my lips part slightly because it was so beautiful. It was almost like a whole other world.

Romeo felt my reaction and smiled smugly, almost as if he knew how gorgeous this place was and how taken I'd be.

It was an older neighborhood. I knew because all the trees were huge and mature. Their branches stretched far into the sky and over the street we drove down. The green leaves created a canopy over the road, like we were driving through a tunnel created by Mother Nature.

Hints of sunlight filtered through the branches as the leaves gently fluttered in the breeze. A sidewalk lined both sides of the street. It was inviting and made me want to get out of the car and walk along it while staring at the manicured lawns that stretched right up to its edge.

This wasn't a cookie cutter neighborhood. Every house looked different than the one beside it; each had its own character and style. But instead of everything looking mismatched and kind of thrown together, it appeared opulent and natural.

We passed by a white colonial style with a red front door. The columns on the porch were regal and strong. The house beside it was red brick with a front porch lined with flower boxes overflowing with beautiful blooms in every color.

The driveways were all paved meticulously, the curb appeal of every home inviting.

I had a sudden image of children carrying oversized bags running across the lawns, dressed in Halloween costumes, to ring the doorbells and yell trick-or-treat!

This was the kind of neighborhood I saw on TV. The kind I thought didn't really exist anymore. Sure, I'd been down lots of nice streets; Romeo lived on one of them.

But there was something about this neighborhood, this very street, that spoke to me on a deeper level.

The car slowed, and I tore my gaze away from the passing scenery to glance at Romeo. He lifted our locked hands and kissed the back of mine.

"What are we doing here?" I asked. "Are we meeting someone?"

"Something like that," he murmured and then released my hand so he could guide the Hellcat into a driveway.

I wasn't a girl who cared much about things. I knew Romeo had money. I knew he was used to beautiful places, clothes, and a certain quality of life. He never acted like a snob or a spoiled brat.

I was staying at his house over the summer. I guess I could admit I was used to being around all his nice things. I was used to his house and his car.

That being said, I wasn't often impressed. I wasn't often taken with something I thought was gorgeous. Except right now.

The house we pulled up to was incredibly gorgeous. I couldn't help but stare out the windshield to take in its charm.

It was built of stone—natural-looking, all in tones of tan and brown. It wasn't the kind of stone that was perfectly cut to fit together; it literally looked like it was unearthed from the ground and pieced onto the house like a puzzle being fit together.

It had large white-framed windows, the kind with panes that would collect a dusting of snowflakes in the winter. The front door was wide and painted a cheerful shade of yellow with the house numbers in polished gold on display right in the center.

The porch was simple concrete. Steps rose up out of the ground into a large platform in front of the door. I imagined pots of flowers everywhere, lining each of the steps and framing the entrance.

The garage door we parked in front of was freshly painted white, and large green plants and bushes lined the walkway that led to the front porch.

"Who lives here?" I asked, my voice sounding a little breathy.

"You like it?" Romeo asked.

I nodded, still taking in the stone exterior and noticing a thick covering of deep-green ivy covering the far garage wall.

"It looks like it belongs in a storybook."

His grin was quick and very pleased. Before I could ask him for more details, he bolted out of the car. "Come on."

I followed behind him, scrambling to keep up as he jogged to the front door. Before I got there, he swung it open and motioned for me to come inside.

"We can't just walk into someone else's house!" I told him. "What's gotten into you?"

"If you don't wanna walk in, I guess I'll have to carry ya," he quipped. "It's probably the way I'm supposed to do it anyway."

"What?" I asked, bewildered.

He scooped me up, cradling me against his chest, and carried me through the front door, kicking it shut behind him.

"Wow," I said, taking in the open space, the shiny dark floor, and the sunlight that filled the entire main level.

He walked around quickly, still carrying me like I weighed nothing at all. If I hadn't been distracted by the beautiful fireplace, bookshelves in the corner, and the kitchen that looked like it belonged in a magazine, I would have told him carrying me was bad for his arm.

Before I knew it, he was backtracking through the place and heading up the stairs, which were near the front door.

"Romeo!" I stiffened. What the hell was he doing?

He chuckled and kissed my forehead like he thought it was cute I was appalled we were invading someone else's house.

"It's four bedrooms," he said. "They're all pretty big. There's three and a half bathrooms too."

The hallway up here was carpeted. It looked soft and clean, but I couldn't really say how soft it was because he was still carrying me.

"You can put me down," I reminded him.

"Wanna see the master?"

I did. I wanted to see every inch of this place. "Sure," I said. I mean, why the hell not? We were already up here.

His teeth flashed and a satisfied look crossed his face.

We stopped in front of a white door, and Romeo pushed it open.

I gasped when he stepped inside.

It was a huge room, bigger than the dorm room Ivy and I shared. Bigger than the room Romeo had at his house. But the size wasn't why I gasped.

In the center was a huge bed, definitely a king. It had a tall upholstered headboard, the tufted kind, that was covered in a soft, light-colored fabric.

The rails along the mattress and box springs were also upholstered, and the entire thing sat high off the ground. I mean, seriously, like the mattress probably came up to my waist.

The rest of the room was empty, but the bed was completely done. It was covered in white bedding, the sheets and blanket and comforter folded back halfway down the center. White fluffy pillows lined the top and filled the space, but even the amount couldn't keep the headboard from being the focal point.

Stretched across the end of the bed was a gray blanket so soft I wanted to wrap it around my shoulders.

"We shouldn't be in here," I said, unable to tear my eyes away from the bed. "This is someone's home, their space."

I started to turn, to backtrack out of the room, but Romeo caught my hand. "Maybe you should look at the note on the bed."

The note?

I swung back around and my eyes fastened on a white envelope lying on the corner of the bed.

I went forward and scooped it up. My fingers brushed against the blanket, reveling in the plush feel.

I glanced at him before pulling out the card inside. He nodded.

Carefully, I slid out a white piece of paper. Scrawled in handwriting that had become incredibly familiar were two words.

Welcome Home

My eyes shot to his. I turned the note around, holding it out for him to see.

"I already know what it says." His tone was amused.

"You wrote this?" I asked.

Yes, I was a smart girl.

But right now, my brain was working extremely slow.

A smile curved his mouth and he closed the distance between us, slipping an arm around my waist and pulling me flush against him. The card was still in my hand and it flattened against his chest, the words facing out as I stared at them some more.

"This is your house?" I asked, looking up.

He shook his head.

I felt my brow crease. If it wasn't his house . . .

"It's ours."

My fingers tightened on the note. "Ours?"

"For the next year anyway."

"A year . . ." I echoed, still trying to take it all in.

"After that, if this place still puts that look on your face, I'll buy it. Hell, looking at you now, I sort of regret not just buying it outright."

"You rented this house?"

Amusement lit his eyes. He reached up and covered my hand resting against his chest. "Now, baby, I know this is very exciting, but try and keep up."

He totally rented this house!

I pulled back and paced to the large window taking up the far wall. I tried not to be distracted by the way this room overlooked the backyard and its wooden fence.

"Why on earth would you rent a house? You're leaving next week."

"I still need a place to live," he drawled.

I swung around. "You have a place. A very nice place."

He shrugged one shoulder. "That's not our place."

I sputtered a bit. "I'll be moving back to the dorm."

He shook his head. "I don't want you at the dorm."

My eyes narrowed on his face. "Romeo . . ." I warned. He better not be trying to pull this overprotective bossy-pants attitude.

"Baby," he said soft and took a step toward me.

I help up my hand. "Stay right there," I said, firm.

He seemed rather entertained by my order but kept prowling closer. "You don't want me to stay all the way over here."

Yes. Yes, I did. Because the second he was within touching distance, my resolve would crumble and I'd be putty in his very large, very skilled hands.

I backed up a step, and his smile turned wolfish.

"Hear me out, love," he murmured, capturing me around the waist. Instead of pulling me in, he turned me so we were both facing out, looking over the sprawling green lawn dotted with large trees. I bet in the fall they would be multicolored and stunning.

His chin rested on my shoulder, and I gave in. I was such a sucker for him.

"I don't want to leave," he began, and I sucked in a breath, about to turn. He tightened his arms and held me where I stood. "The closer the day on the calendar gets, the more and more I wish my dream of the NFL hadn't come so fast. Having you at my place this summer, all to myself, has been better than free beer at a club."

I rolled my eyes but didn't say anything.

"I can't let you go, Rim. It's bad enough I have to leave, that I won't be able to see you every day. I won't be the first one to touch you in the morning or the last one to see you at night. I don't want you back at the dorms, in a place that's temporary, in a world that isn't ours. When I lie down at night, I want to know you're in our bed. In our house. I want you to be surrounded by me, even if I'm not physically here."

"Oh, Romeo." I sighed. His words painted a picture in my heart. I saw it clearly as he spoke. Longing, deep and hard, filled me. I wanted that, too.

I spun in the circle of his arms; my hands linked behind his neck. "I don't need a house to be surrounded by you. I don't need anything at all for that."

"I want to do this, baby. Please don't fight me on it."

So badly I wanted to say yes. To give in and let him have his way.

I pulled back. He let me go. I felt his eyes on me, even with my back turned.

"I can't afford this house, Romeo."

"Yes, you can."

I lifted an eyebrow. "Last time I looked, my paycheck wasn't that much."

"Good thing my paycheck is pretty fat."

I fisted my hands and put them on my hips.

He groaned. "Are we gonna have this conversation again?"

"Well, clearly, you didn't hear me the last hundred times," I muttered.

"I hear just fine. I just don't like what you say."

I snorted.

"I have money. That probably isn't gonna change, baby. That means you have money now, too. I know you don't care about it. Hell," he said and rubbed a hand down his face, "I know money complicates things."

I knew he was talking about my father and all his gambling and money issues.

"But it doesn't have to with us. I'm gonna take care of you. That's the way it's gonna be. I'm gonna make sure you have a safe place to live, a place where you can be at the end of every day. I'm gonna make sure you have everything, Rim. And it's not just for you; it's for me, too. I won't be able to play, to concentrate on my game, if I'm worried about you. If you won't let me take care of you for you, then let me do it for me."

It was almost disgusting how pretty his words were.

But damn if they didn't make me melt inside anyway.

"That's the way it's gonna be, huh?"

Whatever he heard in my voice made him smile like he'd won the lottery.

I pinned him with a hard look, and a little of the smugness left his eyes. "I'm gonna help with the bills," I said, hoping to heaven the utilities on a place like this didn't give me a rash every month.

He nodded.

"And I'll do the shopping and cleaning."

His mouth flattened like the idea of me doing ordinary chores offended him. I crossed my arms over my chest and dared him to say anything.

He sighed. "Fine."

"Do we need such a big place?" I asked, doubt still in my voice.

"I was thinking maybe we could ask B and Ivy to move in, too."

My chest filled with happiness. "Really!"

He grinned. It was a crooked, boyish smile. "Yep. She needs somewhere to keep that rat you made her fall in love with."

"Prada is not a rat," I growled.

He didn't argue, but he didn't agree either. "Besides, after everything that went down last semester, I think she'd probably like not having to live on campus."

So this wasn't just for me. It was for her, too. Emotion pierced my heart at Romeo's thoughtfulness. He knew what a rough time Ivy had last semester, what a rough time I still suspected she was having and trying to hide.

"I thought you might want to keep her as a roommate."

I nodded eagerly. I was dreading who I was going to be paired with this semester.

That made me realize . . ."I have to live on campus. My scholarship . . ."

"Already taken care of."

"You arranged for me to live off campus and keep my scholarship?"

He held out his arms like he could do anything. I was beginning to think he could.

"What about Braeden?" I asked.

"What about him?" Romeo shrugged.

"Does he know about this?"

"Not yet. But he'll move in. There's no way he'll let you two live by yourself."

Ah, so he was moving in a bodyguard in the form of my big bro.

"You'll be here a lot, too." My teeth sank into my lower lip as that homesick feeling turned my tummy. "Won't you?"

He rushed across the room and took my face in his hands. "Every chance I get."

"Okay." I sighed. The warmth from his palms seeped into my cheeks and made my eyes heavy.

He made a whooping sound, lifting me off my feet and tossing me on the bed. I sank into the blankets instantly and sighed.

"Is this our bed?" I asked, really hoping it was.

"You like?"

"Mm-hmm."

"Then, yes." He lowered himself so he was lying on top of me.

"How did you have time to do all this today?" I asked, running my fingers through his hair.

"Bed was already here. I just went out and bought all the stuff that goes on it. Mattress cover, sheets, blankets, pillows . . ."

"I love you," I whispered.

His eyes crinkled at the corners. "I was gonna fill the room with candles, but I really thought you'd be a lot harder to convince, and I was running out of time."

"It's perfect." I sighed and pulled him close. "I really do love this house," I said against his neck.

"Thank fuck," he murmured and pulled back. "I was afraid you'd be pissed I picked out our house without you."

"As long as you're here, the rest is just details."

He kissed me.

"Of course," I said when he pulled back, "you do have really good taste."

"Hells yeah."

"How much did this cost you, Romeo?"

"Doesn't matter. You already said you'd live here."

I groaned. That meant way too much.

"Should we call B?" I asked. "Ivy?"

He shook his head slow, the blue in his eyes filling with desire. "Later."

"Later?"

"I got one week in this house with you, baby. We need to fill it with pieces of us so when I leave, it already feels like home."

"You are my home, Romeo."

He kissed me repeatedly. In between each one, he spoke. "First the bed." Kiss. "Then maybe the hallway." Kiss. "The kitchen for sure." Kiss. "The living room . . ."

I moved restlessly beneath him, the hard length of his cock teasing me as we kissed.

"Even before we move in the furniture, you're gonna see me in every room."

"Romeo." I groaned and wrapped my legs around his waist.

"Welcome home, baby," he whispered against my lips.

"Welcome home," I whispered back.

We didn't speak again for a long time.

HASHTAG SERIES BONUS SCENE #3

STARRING THE FAB FOUR

BY CAMBRIA HEBERT

This scene takes place one month after Nova is born.
*Brand new scene—exclusive to #Hookup!

RIMMEL

NERVOUS ENERGY SKITTERED AROUND THE interior of the car like a basket of bouncy balls that had been dropped onto a hard surface.

I dared a quick glance away from the road to Ivy, who was riding shotgun. There was a tissue clutched in her hand, but her eyes were dry. At least she wasn't crying.

That was something, yes?

A couple tears spilled over when we first backed out of the garage and then drove through the gates of the property, but beyond that, none had fallen. Her face was drawn, though, her forehead wrinkled and eyes wide.

I didn't point out the tight grip she used on the poor tissue or the fact that her knee was bobbing up and down so fast it actually made me a little car sick to look at it.

She caught me giving her a worried look and tried to smile. "I'm fine. Really."

That was a lie, and we both knew it.

I wasn't fine, and Nova was only my niece. I couldn't even imagine how hard it was for Ivy to leave her little baby for the first time ever.

Granted, it was only a short little time out. A chance to get out of the house and "relax." I had to admit, though, this was frankly the furthest thing from relaxing.

The drive to the boutique Ivy used to practically run over by the Alpha U campus was longer than it used to be since we didn't live so close to the university. We were silent most of the way. Ivy checked her phone (which was also in a death grip), and I kept glancing at the dash, calculating how long we'd been gone.

When the familiar street finally came into view, both of us let out an audible sigh of relief. Our eyes darted to each other, and then we both started to giggle.

"Who would have thought that getting me to go shopping would be such a hardship?" Ivy quipped.

I giggled. "It's definitely not something I would have ever predicted."

"She changed me," Ivy confided as I drove past the boutique and the full parking along the street. "Having Nova completely realigned my life."

"I know. You're such a good mom to her." I agreed and pulled into a parking lot at the corner of the block.

Once the Range Rover was parked, I turned toward her. Ivy was different now, calmer than she used to be. More . . . confident in herself. Most people would probably think that was the stupidest thing they ever heard. Ivy not confident? *scoff*

But that was what people beyond our family didn't understand. They didn't get to see her many layers and all the details I'd learned about her since the day we'd moved into the same dorm room.

Ivy was gorgeous, always pulled together, bubbly, popular, and well liked. The YouTube channel she started was gaining popularity fast because she had the kind of personality that drew people in.

No one would have guessed she wasn't always so confident, that a lot of it was a screen for her vulnerabilities.

Marrying Braeden and then giving birth to Nova seemed to bring her into herself more. It was just like she said. Her life was realigned now. Other people (outside our family) didn't factor in so much, and not caring about that was freeing for her.

"Do you miss shopping? Working at the boutique and getting out?" I asked gently. Since having Nova a little over a month ago, she'd barely left the compound.

Frankly, I hadn't either. With Romeo and Braeden away more than half that time due to games (which B was very growly about), the only place I went was to work and the grocery store. The rest of my time was at home with Ivy and Nova.

Babies were a lot of work, and I got a serious crash course in taking care of one.

Ivy made a sound. "Sometimes," she said honestly. "But not nearly as much as I thought I might. When Nova's a little older, I'll go out more and take her with me."

I grinned. "You never know. B and Romeo might be having the time of their life."

Ivy made a rude sound. "I still can't believe we left her alone with them." Her lower lip wobbled. "I miss her."

I reached across the seat and patted her hand. "Why don't you call them before we go inside?"

Ivy already had B's number pulled up on her phone screen. The second I made the suggestion, she hit the call button and then put on the speaker.

"It's been twenty minutes, Blondie," B answered, his voice exasperated.

"What's wrong?" Ivy perked up instantly.

"Wrong?" Braeden wondered. "Why do you think something's wrong?"

"You sound upset." She worried, wringing her hands and glancing at me.

My brother made a rude sound. "I'm upset you think I can't handle my own daughter for twenty minutes."

"But I miss her!" Ivy wailed instantly, her voice breaking. Unshed tears spilled over, and she lifted the tissue to her eyes instantly.

Braeden let out a low string of curses.

"Not in front of the baby!" we both yelled.

"Romeo is holding her," Braeden informed us.

"Why aren't you holding her?" Ivy demanded. "Is she okay?"

Braeden made a sound. His tone was defensive when he spoke. "Do you think I'd just hand her off to Rome if she wasn't?"

In the background, Romeo called out, "She's fine!"

"I handed her to him because you were calling me." B pointed out.

"Oh," Ivy said, sniffling. "Of course."

Braeden sighed rather loudly. I could almost picture him rubbing his hand over his face. "Baby, are you crying?"

"No," Ivy wailed, and it was totally not convincing.

"You know I don't like it when you cry," he grumbled, his voice no longer angry. "She's fine. I swear. All she's done is sleep."

"What if she thinks I abandoned her?" Ivy's voice was small as she dabbed at her eyes.

I held my breath, hoping Braeden kept his sarcastic wisecracks inside for once. He seemed to understand she was truly distraught because his voice remained gentle. "I already told her you'd be back after you got some pretty outfits for Aunt Rimmel to wear for the press."

"You did?"

"Of course I did, baby."

"Did Romeo tell her, too?"

There was a pregnant pause on the other end of the line. "Of course he told her."

"Hells yeah," Romeo called out.

What a bunch of liars. Ha! I didn't bother calling them out, though, because Ivy seemed content to believe Romeo was indeed telling Nova all about her mother.

In actuality, they were probably telling her all about football. And to never date.

"If you need anything—" She began, but B cut her off.

"We're fine, Ives. I got this. She's like a tiny baby. Hell, Prada is bigger than her. Me and Rome can handle one little baby."

Ivy glanced at me, and I rolled my eyes.

"You're with her twenty-four-seven, and I barely get to see her. It's Daddy time. Now go buy a bunch of shit you don't need and let me have my daughter for a couple hours."

"Well, okay." She agreed reluctantly.

He made a gruff sound. "Good."

"See ya later, princess!" Romeo called out in the background. My heart thumped just a little quicker at the sound of his voice.

"Bye," Ivy said, still gripping the phone like she was dialing 9–1-1.

I almost started the car up and went home. I could just wear what I had to my upcoming appearances with Romeo. It wasn't like I actually cared anyway.

"Baby." Braeden's smooth, low voice filled the car. Ivy's hand tightened, then relaxed around the phone.

"Yeah?"

"I love you."

Her eyes closed for long moments. When she reopened them, they were no longer filled with tears. "I love you, too."

"I'll call if I need anything." He assured, trying to make her feel better. Then in true Braeden style, he just had to add, "But I won't. Babies are easy!"

He disconnected the line, and Ivy glanced up at me. "He's such a moron."

"I can't say I disagree."

Ivy grinned. "I do love him, though."

My lips curved up. That call with my BBFL did just the trick to make her feel better. As idiotic as B and Romeo were, they were also reliable, solid, and entirely lovable. They had a way of always knowing when to reassure us.

"Shopping?"

"Of course," she chirped. "Suddenly, I feel like buying something. I mean, it's been forever since I've bought anything that wasn't online."

"Well then," I announced as we both got out of the car, "let's go!"

# # #

ROMEO

HOW THE HELL DID SOMETHING so tiny make so much chaos?

Not even five minutes after B hung up the phone with Ivy, all hell broke loose.

Or rather . . . little Nova made a liar out of her daddy and uncle. Not that we would admit defeat.

Hells no.

We were two grown men. Two big football players who took tackles, won NFL games, and could bench press more than our own weight.

A baby was nothing.

"Why won't she stop crying, man?" Braeden stressed.

He was pacing in front of the fireplace, holding the tiny bundle against his chest, gingerly supporting her, bouncing her lightly. His palm was larger than her head, but damn did she have a set of lungs on her.

I was standing nearby, too agitated to even sit on the couch. Rubbing a hand over the back of my neck, I glanced at her. She was wiggly and screaming in his arms.

"Maybe she needs a new diaper," I suggested.

Braeden lifted her and smelled her bottom. "Nah. She's good."

The baby continued to cry, becoming more insistent. I watched B turn her around in his arms, cradling her against his chest so he could stare down into her face. I couldn't help but notice the bead of sweat of his forehead.

"Hey now," he crooned, trying not to sound stressed the hell out. "Tell Daddy what's the matter."

Nova paused for just a fraction at the sound of his voice before turning her head and screaming some more.

"What the hell did you do to her, Rome!" B demanded, pinning me with a glare.

"Me!" I gasped.

"She was fine 'til I let you hold her!" He accused.

"Women love me," I refuted. To prove the point, I went over to stand directly in front of her. I leaned down and caressed her cheek with my finger. Nova turned toward it like she wanted to eat it.

"She's hungry!" Braeden surmised.

"Ivy did say something about a bottle." I remembered.

Between us, Nova screamed some more.

"Get the bottle, man!" B said, totally stressing out.

I rushed to the kitchen. I pulled a bottle out of the fridge and turned to rush back to the living room, but B was coming into the kitchen with the fussing baby.

"Here." I thrust it at him.

B took it and frowned. "This is cold. I'm not feeding my kid cold milk!"

"Put it in the micro?" I asked.

B shrugged. We went toward the microwave and popped it open to put the bottle inside. The second the door sprang open, we saw a huge note hanging in the opening.

DO NOT put a bottle in here.

"Why the hell not?" I wondered.

Braeden growled and retreated to the fridge where Ivy had hung a long list of directions we told her we didn't need.

Braeden scanned them while trying to shush the baby.

"Hold my daughter, Rome," he said, propelling her at me. "And don't make her cry worse."

I took her, gently folding her against my chest. Her face was turning red and her little fists were shaking. "Man, you better do something," I told him.

"Hey there, princess," I told her softly. "We're gonna get you a nice bottle."

Across the room, Braeden had plugged in some appliance that you set the bottle in and it gently warmed it.

"How do you know when it's done?" B asked after what felt like forever.

I was rocking the baby back and forth. She was making so much racket Prada and Darcy (Rim's adoptive dog) were sitting at my feet with their ears pulled back, staring up at the baby.

A loud beeping filled the room, and B lunged at the bottle. He grabbed it up and carried it over. The outside was damp.

"Here," he said, thrusting it at me.

"Check it on your wrist," I told him. "Ivy does that."

"Fuck," B muttered and then dumped out a few drops on the inside of his wrist. He made a face. "It ain't that hot."

Nova gave a yell.

"Maybe she likes it like that," I suggested.

My nerves were frayed. One of the dogs whined.

B reached for his daughter, and I surrendered her willingly. The second the nipple touched her lips, she latched on, and silence permeated the room.

"That gives a new definition to the word hangry," I muttered.

Braeden didn't say anything. He was too intent on Nova, making sure her head was supported and he was holding the bottle right. The dogs started dancing around our feet, and then Murphy sauntered into the kitchen.

"This place is a zoo," I muttered. "C'mon! Out!" I told the dogs, sliding open the doors to the back deck. Both Darcy and Prada just stood there and stared at me.

"Out," I growled.

Darcy lay down.

A black blur darted past me, making me do a double take.

"Murphy!" I roared. The damn cat ran outside! "Fuck!" I swore as I lunged after him. If this cat ran off, Rimmel would be devastated. She'd never forgive me.

And even though I'd never say it out loud, I would be pretty wrecked, too. Rim and I bonded over Murphy. It was in the shelter where I first felt the stirrings of love for her. Seeing her with the one-eyed cat in her lap and my hoodie around her body was a picture I would never, ever forget.

Murphy leapt up on the railing of the deck and stared down.

"No!" I growled, menacing. "Murphy!"

His black body flinched, and he crouched down. Cautiously, I approached. Then all at once, I pounced on him.

He gave a great meow when I pulled him into my chest. His claws dug into my T-shirt and pricked the skin on my chest.

"I thought we were bros," I told him. "You trying to get me in trouble?"

He started purring.

I wasn't about to fall for it.

I went back inside and didn't put him down 'til the door was firmly shut. The dogs acted like I'd just got home from an away game, wiggling and leaping all around my feet.

I picked up a nearby toy, gave it a squeak, and threw it into the living room.

They ran off, sounding like a heard of elephants, and I breathed a sigh of relief. Not two seconds later, the sound of something crashing to the floor out in the room filled my ears.

I ignored it.

B was still in the same spot, still holding the bottle up to Nova's mouth.

"Shouldn't you burp her?" I asked, remembering the girls always telling us.

"I'm not taking this damn bottle from her. She'll cry!"

I grimaced. "Good call."

"Dude," I said, looking in the fridge. "I need a beer."

B made a sound of agreement, and I pulled out two sodas instead. We might want beer, but drinking in front of a baby was just wrong.

The dogs came rumbling back into the room, and Darcy dropped the toy at my feet. I threw it again, and they rushed off.

Nova emptied her bottle, and B sat it on the counter and gently put her up on his shoulder to pat her back.

Not two seconds later, Nova let out one hell of a belch.

"Nice!" I said proudly.

Braeden made a face.

"What?"

He turned, showing me his back. "I think she spit up on me."

I laughed. "I think half her bottle is down your back."

"Maybe I should have burped her," he muttered.

I reached for her so he could pull off his shirt and drop it onto the floor. Nova cuddled into my chest, and my heart warmed. She was so tiny, but I loved her so much.

Rocking a little back and forth, I watched B wash his hands at the sink. Two seconds later, my chest was covered with the other half of her bottle.

"Ah, man." I groaned.

Nova started fussing again.

"It's okay, baby." I promised her, pulling her body away from the spit up.

The dogs ran back into the room and sat down to stare at the baby.

"Come on now, Critter," B said, taking her. "Don't be upset. Daddy and Uncle Rome don't mind a little throw up. It's okay," he murmured, hugging her close.

Her cries quieted, so Braeden carried her into the living room. Both dogs followed along behind him.

I pulled off my shirt and dropped it on the floor, then washed my hands and finished off my soda.

"Rome!" Braeden yelled from the other room, his voice urgent.

I rushed to see what was wrong.

"Dude, she exploded!"

"What?" I asked. He was leaning back on the couch, the baby against him. He was holding both arms out in the air like he didn't know what to do.

"Oh, it's bad," he said and gagged.

Nova made a little sound, almost like she was happy.

I came forward, noticed the stuff oozing out from the edges of her diaper and onesie. It was smeared on B's stomach.

"That's nasty," I said, wrinkling my nose. "I didn't know babies could make that smell."

"Me either."

"Maybe we should call Ivy," I suggested.

"Hells no!" he quipped. "I will not admit defeat."

I nodded.

Braeden stood, holding her tight despite the fact she was covered in actual shit. I made a mental note to high-five him for that later.

"Lay out a blanket so I can change her," he instructed.

I did, and he laid the baby out on it and grabbed a handful of baby wipes and cleaned off his chest and stomach.

I laughed under my breath, and he glanced up sharply. "Shit is no laughing matter, Rome!"

I laughed harder.

Nova began kicking her legs around.

"Whoa," B said, moving to grasp her tiny feet. "Don't be flinging it around, Critter."

We both leaned over the baby, focused on getting her cleaned up. I passed him wipe after wipe and held open a bag to toss them into once used. Then we undressed her ('cause you know, the shit and the spit up . . .), and B put a clean diaper on her.

He gazed around, glancing in the basket where Ivy kept diapers and wipes and shit.

"I need some clothes for her."

I looked in the basket, too. There weren't any.

"She has some in her room," B said.

I started to push up. "I'll go."

He slapped a hand over my wrist. "Don't leave me alone with her."

I laughed. "It's a baby."

"And I love her, but she might explode again!"

He was right. She might.

There was a laundry basket on the couch, some folded clothing inside. I reached in and plucked out one of B's T-shirts. It was a Knights one.

B snatched it out of my hand, and he wrapped it around the baby like it was a blanket. After he tucked the ends in, she was swaddled up good.

Nova looked up at Braeden, her blue eyes latching onto his face. He felt her gaze like the sun on a cold day, instantly drawn to her.

The edges of his lips turned up. "I think purple is your color, Critter," he said fondly. When he lifted her, he pressed a kiss to her cheeks and then her head.

She smiled at him.

Braeden tossed his hand out, smacking me in the chest. "You see that!" he whispered excitedly.

"Sure do."

"I knew I was her favorite."

"You have shit on your jeans," I said, dry.

He didn't tear his eyes away from his daughter for long moments. "You can shit on me anytime you want, sweetheart." When he finally looked up, he shucked the jeans right there in the middle of the room. Wearing nothing but a pair of black boxers, he yawned loudly.

Nova started fussing again, and both of us glanced up like a deer in headlights.

Thinking fast, B snatched her pacifier off the table and held it to her lips. She sucked it in and settled down instantly.

"Dude, babies make me tired," he told me.

I agreed.

Braeden reclined back on the sofa. "How the hell does Ivy do this all day?"

"We leave them here all the time by themselves like this," I murmured, equally in awe. It also made me feel kinda guilty.

"We should buy them some diamonds or some shit."

Clearly, B was feeling the same guilt. I made a sound of agreement and sat down on the chair nearby, propping my feet up on the coffee table.

Darcy leapt up beside me, squishing his hairy, not-very-small ass in the space beside me, partially lying on top of me.

I was about to tell him to get down, but he licked me on the chin.

Prada lay in front of the couch near B, and Murphy curled up near my head on the pillow.

B and I started to talk football, but the conversation didn't last very long because we both fell asleep.

#

RIMMEL

"THESE LAST TWO HOURS HAVE literally felt like eternity," Ivy said as I pulled into the garage and hit the button for it to close behind us.

I smiled. "Now you know how I feel every time we go shopping."

Ivy laughed. "Well, we got some good stuff. You're going to be looking fierce for your next few appearances."

"All thanks to you." Seriously. If it weren't for Ivy, I'd be a terrible mess in every picture ever taken of me and Romeo.

"Think they did okay?" Ivy asked as she hurried around the back of the Rover.

"Well, they didn't call for help." I snorted after the words left my mouth. "Like they would."

"I missed her," Ivy said, rushing toward the door and flinging it open.

Inside the mud room, she spun and looked at me, her eyes wide. "Why is it so quiet in here?"

Dropping all the bags right there on the floor, we hurried into the kitchen, where I gasped. It was a complete disaster. Ivy put her hands on her hips and made a sound of distress. She recovered much faster, dismissing it all and heading toward the living room.

I, on the other hand, stared in awe at the clothes on the floor (why were there clothes on the kitchen floor?), empty soda cans, chip crumbs, an empty bottle, a couple dish towels, and the bottle warmer askew and still plugged into the outlet. I went forward to unplug it and noticed there was still water in the bottom of it.

Ivy made a distressed sound, and I forgot about it all and rushed to her side.

"Oh my God!" she whisper-yelled. "Just look at this place!"

I skidded to a stop, and the pair of us stood in awe, looking over the living room where both guys were passed out on the furniture, snoring. They hadn't even heard us come in. The dogs either!

We could have been burglars!

Seeing us now, the two dogs began beating their tails. Prada got up and rushed to Ivy, who spared a moment to drop down and rub the dog behind her ears. Darcy gave a low whine in my direction but didn't move from his sprawled position on Romeo's chest.

I couldn't help but smile at the way Romeo had his arm thrown around the dog.

It was totally charming.

I went over and scratched Darcy behind his ears as I glanced around at Ivy. She straightened and went toward Nova, staring down at her husband and daughter.

The picture they created actually caused a lump to form in my throat. A wistful feeling wrapped around my heart and squeezed at the idea of Romeo someday sleeping on the couch with our child curled into his chest.

"They're everything," Ivy whispered, her voice emotional.

"They really are." I agreed.

Ivy pulled out her phone and snapped a couple pictures of father and daughter snoring away together, then turned her camera on Romeo and Darcy.

"You might have some competition, Rim," Ivy cracked.

I giggled.

Her attention returned back to B and Nova, and it was almost like the sweetness-induced haze in which she saw them vanished.

"What in heavens name is my daughter wearing?" Ivy burst out.

Both guys jolted awake instantly.

"Wha—?" Romeo sprang up.

Braeden's arm came around the baby, who was sleeping, cuddled into his chest. She was barely jolted when he sprang up, immediately ready to protect her.

When he saw it was us, he dropped back against the cushions with a sigh. "Hey, Blondie."

"Braeden James Walker!" Ivy intoned, putting her hands on her hips. "What have you done to my daughter!"

His eyes widened, and he glanced down. "What's wrong with her?"

"She's naked!"

"She is not!" Braeden insisted. "What kind of father do you think I am? No daughter of mine will be showing her girly bits to all the world."

I snorted.

Darcy jumped off the couch, and Romeo caught me around the waist and pulled me into his lap. "Hey, baby," he whispered, nuzzling the side of my neck.

His skin of his bare chest was warm and solid. I pecked a quick kiss on his cheek before glancing back at a stormy Ivy.

"One of your shirts is not clothing, Braeden." Ivy insisted, her words much firmer than the way she reached out for the baby. "Come here, sweetheart," she crooned.

Ivy picked her up and cradled the baby in her arms, her eyes roaming over her like she was making sure she was still in one piece.

Her nose wrinkled. "She smells. Why does she smell?"

"Why are you in your underwear?" I asked Braeden.

"You didn't tell me she could explode," Braeden replied, pinning Ivy with a glare.

"Explode!" She gasped.

"Out of both ends." Romeo agreed with Braeden.

"Is that why you're half dressed, too?" I inquired.

"What in God's name happened in here?" she asked, looking around, her stare (and mine) ultimately landing on a blanket with an open bag filled with dirty baby wipes and a diaper.

"Is that poop on the blanket?" I asked.

"I don't know what you've been feeding my baby, Blondie, but you're doing it wrong," Braeden deadpanned.

Ivy gasped. "What did you just say to me?" In her arms, Nova began to squirm around. "It's okay, baby. Mommy's home."

"We had an issue with the diaper," Romeo explained, trying to help his brother out. "But don't worry. We got her cleaned up."

"And dressed her in a man's T-shirt." Ivy pointed out.

"It's clean," Braeden defended.

Romeo nodded.

"And where is your shirt?" Ivy asked, pinning Romeo with a fiercely blue stare.

"Spit up," he said.

"I suppose you're going to blame the lamp on the floor on the baby, too?" I asked, trying to hide my amusement.

"That was the dog," Braeden said.

Nova started fussing, and Braeden jumped up, rushing to Ivy's side. "She's hungry," Ivy told him.

"How do you know?" he demanded. "She just ate!"

"She eats a lot. She's a baby." Ivy pointed out. "And it sounds like half of it didn't stay in her belly."

"Did you burp her?" I asked Romeo.

"I told him to. He was scared to take the bottle from her."

"She was hangry." B defended.

Romeo nodded sagely. "She was."

"You two are morons!" Ivy announced. Then she glanced down at the baby and smiled. "C'mon, sweetheart, let's get you a bottle."

"Don't forget to heat it up!" Romeo called after her.

She told him to shut it.

Braeden snickered.

I glanced at my brother and lifted my brows. "I thought babies were easy."

"Ah, hell, sis," he muttered.

A few moments later, Ivy came back into the room and sank down beside B on the couch. Both of them stared down at the baby who was happily drinking up her bottle.

"See, baby," Braeden quipped. "Nova loved hanging out with us."

"We're her favorites," Romeo informed us.

"You're my favorite, too," I whispered into his ear. His palm curled around my hip and his lips met mine.

After a quiet moment, Ivy sighed. "I guess she did. You're a good daddy, Braeden. And, Romeo, you're a good uncle."

I nodded, totally agreeing. But I couldn't help but add, "Even if now she needs a bath, actual clothes, and this place will take the rest of the day to clean."

Beneath me, Romeo's chest rumbled with a low laugh.

"You're gonna help us with that, right?" B asked.

Ivy and I laughed.

HASHTAG SERIES BONUS SCENE #4

STARRING ROMEO AND RIMMEL

BY CAMBRIA HEBERT

*This scene takes place present day—after the
completion of the #Hashtag and GearShark series.
Brand new scene—exclusive to #Hookup!

ROMEO

THE ENGINE OF THE HELLCAT purred. It was a sound I loved so much I kept the radio turned down when I drove her. Even though the Cat wasn't as new as she used to be, she still ran like the first day I got her.

The credit for that went to Drew and Trent. Having two gearheads in my family sure kept my favorite car in tip-top shape.

Truth was I didn't get to drive the Hellcat as much as I used to, even though she was still the best car in the garage. Now we needed cars with a hell of a lot more seats. It was worth the tradeoff, though. I wouldn't give up the family Rim and I shared just to get more drive time with my car. The way I saw it, the limited drive time I got just made it that much more special.

And today was definitely special.

The car pulled into the lot, up toward the large building, and swung into a prime parking spot. It was the car; she was magic. I always got the best parking when I drove her.

I put her in park but left the engine running just a little longer, allowing the smooth vibrations of to fill my limbs. Pushing the sunglasses up on my head I turned toward Rim, who was riding shotgun.

She glanced at me and smiled. A long, thick braid fell over her shoulder, and her hand rubbed lovingly at her round belly.

God, she was stunning. Unequivocally. Even after all this time, my eyes still only saw her. To me, Rimmel was the definition of beauty; no one else would ever hold a candle to her.

Ever.

Reaching across the center of the car, I palmed her belly. "How's number three?" I asked fondly.

She laughed. "Happy." Her hand moved over mine, sandwiching it between hers and our third child.

"I don't know how he could be anything but," I murmured. "That's some prime real estate he's occupying."

"He?" She lifted her eyebrow.

"Or she." I corrected. "You know I don't care."

"I know." She leaned forward and puckered her lips for a kiss.

Chuckling, I met her halfway, pressing against her supple mouth. The spark between us was well-known by know. It was always there and always my most anticipated feeling.

What was meant to be a quick kiss changed the second our lips met. With a low growl, I leaned forward, wrapping my free hand around the back of her neck and tugging her even closer. She sighed, and my mouth dove against her parted lips, sliding my tongue past the barrier.

I made out with my wife right there in the parking lot, without thought to anyone who might see. Let them look. Loving her wasn't something I would ever hide.

The press didn't bother us as much anymore, not the way they used to when we first got married and when Blue was born. Eventually, hotter news stories came around, celebrity drama and scandals. It was an epic relief not having to be scared every time my wife left the house. Not seeing our faces on the covers of magazines when we went to the store to buy diapers.

Granted, the press still loved us. Of course they would. I was like a fine wine. I only got better with age.

And my stats only got better. The Knights was the pride of the state, a team that barely lost and pulled out some plays that would sit on record books for a long time to come.

Not only that, but I had a hella-hot wife and I made some good-looking kids.

Easing back from our kiss, I relished the way Rim's lips clung to mine just a little bit longer, as if ending the contact was something she hated.

Tugging on the end of her braid, I watched her with heated eyes as she sucked her lower lip into her mouth and then smiled up at me.

"You're more relaxed this time around," I said. "This baby is being good to you."

"They all have been good to me," she rebutted. She would never ever say otherwise. Rim loved all our kids exactly the same. Fiercely.

I chuckled. "I know, but this one is different."

"Fourth time's a charm?" she quipped.

I grinned. Four pregnancies. This would be our fourth child (but the third one we would get to raise; we both still counted Evie because she was our first and we would always love her). "Maybe it is a girl," I murmured. "Maybe that's why you're more relaxed."

"Maybe," she said, caressing her belly again. "Or maybe I'm just more confident my body can do this."

My heart squeezed a little. Hearing those words from her felt like the winning touchdown in a rough game. Some days I doubted I would ever hear them. The loss of our first child was something Rim still carried with her, still ghosted in the back of her head with every new baby we made together.

"You can," I murmured, leaning down to put my forehead against hers. "I'm so damn proud of you, baby. I love you so much."

She caressed the side of my face with her hand. "I'm proud of you, too, Romeo. I thought I won the lottery when I got you, but it keeps getting better. You keep giving me more of you."

I kissed her forehead and pulled back. "Baby, I'll give you as many babies as you want. You know that."

My power to say no to this woman was practically whittled down to nothing. Hell, we had two sons, five dogs (counting Ivy's Prada), a cat, and a new baby on the way. Our house was chaos. I loved every fucking second of it.

"We need to go in. We're going to be late!" she said, glancing at the dash.

I got out and jogged around the side of the Cat and grabbed the door as she pushed it open. Her tiny frame pushed out of the sports car and stood. I didn't move back, so her body brushed against mine when she stepped forward and I slammed the door behind her.

Rim tugged at the white, gauzy top that floated around her belly, then surrendered her hand to mine.

"So?" she asked as we walked into the building. "What do you think? Boy or girl?"

We were finding out the gender of the baby today during her ultrasound. Something else that was different about this pregnancy. Rim refused to find out with our sons. They were both surprises on the day they arrived.

I was surprised when she told me she wanted to find out. But I went with it. Like I said, I hardly ever refuse my wife. She was calmer with this baby, more peaceful. She seemed content and unafraid the baby would be taken like Evie.

She glowed from within—something she always did, pregnant or not—but this time, the glow was a little brighter. I was drawn to her like a moth to a flame. I was also grateful. So fucking grateful she could enjoy this pregnancy without worrying herself near to death.

"I don't know, Rim. I make some pretty good sons," I said.

She laughed. "I can't argue with that. Blue and Asher are definitely spitting images of their daddy."

I grunted with pride. She was right. Both of them had blond hair and blue eyes. Both of them got away with everything and anything in our house. Add B's son Jax into the mix, and we had three strong-willed and curious boys running around all the time.

The only one in our entire family that could keep them in line was Nova.

Their teenage years were definitely going to be interesting.

A five-year-old, two three-year-olds, and Asher who was two. In just a few short months, we'd have another one.

"How would you feel about a girl?" I asked Rim, my voice hushed as we went through the long hallway of the office.

She was quiet a moment. Her head lifted and her eyes met mine. The thought of a girl was always slightly bittersweet because of Evie. "I think I would like that."

The door to the doctor's office came into view, and I reached around my wife to pull it open.

Girl or boy, it really didn't matter. As long as he or she was healthy, neither of us would care.

I had to admit, though, I was kinda excited to find out.

# # #

RIMMEL

THE JELLY STUFF THEY SQUIRTED on my showing belly was cold. I recoiled from it, and Romeo frowned but then instantly turned accusing eyes toward the tech.

I grabbed his hand and squeezed. He glanced at me, and I shook my head.

I could handle cold jelly. He didn't need to make a scene.

The years didn't mellow Romeo's protective nature toward me. If anything, he got worse and worse. Every time I thought there was no way he could be more overprotective, he went and proved me wrong.

"Are you wanting to know the sex this time?" the tech asked us, a woman in her late twenties and dressed in green scrubs.

I glanced at Romeo and nodded.

"Yep," he answered. "Our first time finding out this way."

"How exciting!" she said and pressed the end of the wand to my lower belly. I showed a lot faster this time around. My stomach was already round and popped out. It was because this was baby number three; my stomach muscles weren't as tight as before.

Either that or this baby was going to be gigantic.

Glancing over at Romeo, I grimaced. Having a gigantic baby wasn't exactly out of the realm of possibility. After all, his daddy was a football god.

"You okay, Smalls?" he asked, concern darkening his eyes. The chair he was in made a scraping sound against the floor as he scooted closer to the bed I was reclined on.

"I'm good." I promised. "Just hoping this baby isn't a giant like his daddy."

He laughed.

The sound of the baby's rapid heartbeat filled the room. Tears filled my eyes and happiness squeezed my heart. "There he is!" I said, reaching out for Romeo's hand. His closed around mine instantly, and his lips pressed against the back.

"The heartbeat is nice and strong," the tech told us. "Sounds perfect."

"How's the baby?" I asked, familiar worry and anxiety creeping into my joy. Romeo was right when he pointed out I seemed different this pregnancy. I was more relaxed, but that didn't mean I still didn't worry.

"Everything is looking wonderful," she said, staring at the screen. "See for yourself." She turned the monitor toward us.

The image of our child greeted us. "Oh," I said, tears spilling over my cheeks. "So beautiful."

Romeo was quiet, so I forced my eyes away from the image to glance at him. "Romeo?"

He was staring at the screen, love in his eyes. "She's perfect."

"She?" I said, surprise in my voice. It was the first time Romeo had ever called this baby a she. With two sons at home, we sort of got used to calling the baby a he.

"That's a baby girl, Rim," he said, still staring at the monitor. "I just know it. She's just like you."

"Like me?" I said, turning back toward the baby. "You can't possibly know that."

He made a sound. "Oh, I know. That baby right there has an angelic heart, just like you. I can feel it."

That might have been the sweetest thing he'd ever said to me, and Romeo was very good with words.

I glanced at the technician. "Can you tell the sex?"

She smiled and nodded. "He's right. It's a girl."

Romeo laughed. A happy laugh filled with so much affection.

I burst into tears. Not the silent ones I'd cried earlier, but the sobby kind that made a girl look like a mess.

"Rim," Romeo said, standing from his chair and leaning over me. "Baby, it's okay."

My arms wound around him, and I pulled him in so I could bury my face in his neck. "You gave me another baby girl," I whispered. "Another daughter."

Romeo kissed the side of my head, then pulled back to wipe the tears off my face. "Are you happy?"

"So happy."

"You two are about a cute as they come," the tech said, and we both looked up. She was standing there with the wand in her hand, waiting. "But how about we get some more pictures of that little girl?"

"Oh yes!" I gasped, pushing Romeo back. "I want extra pictures!"

"Well, the standard—" she began to say, but Romeo cut her off, his voice unforgiving.

"I don't care about the standard. Print my wife extra pictures. I'll pay for them."

In the end, I got my pictures. Fifteen of them. And we got to see every inch of our daughter the ultrasound could capture.

She looked perfectly healthy, and so did the parts of my body that cradled her.

Afterward, Romeo took me to get a strawberry milkshake, my newest craving.

"Maybe we should call her strawberry," Romeo quipped with amusement as I sucked it through the straw and made noises of appreciation.

I released the straw and laid my head against his shoulder. His arm, thrown across the back of the booth we were seated in, dropped down and held me tightly.

"I want to name her London."

I felt his stare. "You already have a name?"

I smiled and nodded. "London Rose Anderson."

"London, like the place?" he said thoughtfully.

"My favorite place we've been. That city was so romantic. Do you remember those nights we spent there?"

"Oh, baby, those are nights I won't ever forget," he half growled.

I smiled. "Rose was my mother's middle name."

"London Rose is beautiful, Rim. It's perfect."

"Romeo?" I asked, tilting my head back to stare up at him. "Did you see on the monitor it was a girl before the tech told us? Is that how you knew?"

He shook his head adamantly, the overly long blond hair flopping over his ears. I stared as he brought his free hand up and rubbed over the scruff on his jaw. Over the years, he got in the habit of not shaving so much during the off season.

It was sexy.

In fact, Romeo just seemed to increase in sex appeal the older he got. His athletic body was honed, his face seemed more carved out, and the scruff made his jaw even more square. And his confidence . . . it literally oozed from every pore, even when he slept.

He was a man totally at ease in his skin, in his life, and it showed.

Women still camped out in front of the stadium, in the stands at games, hell, even outside his hotel rooms. I didn't like it. Who would? But I knew those women didn't matter. They had a better chance at meeting Santa Claus than they did at even getting a second of Romeo's attention.

"I told you," he said, answering my question. "I felt it." His hand went to my stomach and caressed. "I can already feel her heart. She's just like you, Rim. She's an angel."

"Someone already has her daddy wound around her finger." My heart sang with love.

"My baby girl," he mused. "A mini of her mother, the woman who literally owns every beat of my heart." His blue eyes blinked, refocusing on mine. "Oh, I'm totally wrapped."

"I love you," I whispered, tears filling my eyes again.

He kissed me softly. "Finish your milkshake, Smalls."

"You think Trent and Drew are okay?" I asked as I sipped.

Romeo laughed. "I don't know, baby. The last time they watched the boys, it took Drew three days to put his tools back in the right place."

I laughed.

Our little boys were naughty. But oh, they were so sweet.

"I want a few more minutes alone with you before we go save them," Romeo told me, and I snuggled into his side again.

Moments alone with Romeo were a lot harder to come by these days. Really, though, it didn't matter because any moment I was with him was special.

The sound of his phone vibrating in the pocket of his jeans made me groan. "I hope Asher didn't throw something else in the toilet." I half laughed.

Romeo laughed as he dug the phone out of his pocket. "That boy acts like Braeden."

My half laugh blossomed into a full one.

"Speaking of," Romeo murmured, then answered the call. "B, what's up?"

He listened for a moment, then replied. "Everything's good. We stopped to get a milkshake." He chuckled. "You know it."

I felt my eyes narrow. B was probably making fun of me for my newest craving. What a butthead.

Romeo's eyes slid to mine. Then he sighed. He pressed the phone against my ear. "B wants to say hi."

"Baby sis!" His voice boomed into my ear. "How ya feeling after the appointment?"

I smiled. "Hey, BBFL. I'm good. Baby looks great."

"You find out if we're getting another boy?"

"Yep, we found out this time."

"Well!" he demanded when I didn't offer any more information.

"Well, we'll tell you when we get home."

"That's cold, sis. Treating your brother that way."

I laughed.

"I'm glad everything's good. Just wanted to hear it from you."

"Love you," I told him.

B was almost as overprotective of me as Romeo, especially when I was pregnant. All the guys in our family were. They were a bunch of cavemen. Still, it was sweet that B would call to make sure I was okay after our appointment. He was a good big brother.

"Times two," he replied, and Romeo pulled the phone back.

"You convinced?" he rumbled into the line. Whatever B said made him grunt.

He was silent a few minutes longer. I felt his gaze come down to me. I swallowed some of the sweet treat and glanced up. His eyes were intense.

"I thought that was later this week?" he spoke. After a pause, he said, "Totally done?"

I listened to him exchange a few more words with B. Then he said, "Tell them to keep their drawers on."

Well, that was odd. Who was trying to take off their pants?

"Yeah, we're on our way." His eyes moved to me again, then away. "I'll talk to her."

The call ended, and I set the milkshake aside and poked him in the stomach. "What was that about?"

Romeo hesitated, then tugged on my side braid again. His blue eyes held a note of wariness as he gazed down. "The pool."

I made a face.

The pool.

#

ROMEO

WE BUILT OUR FAMILY COMPOUND with a lot of bells and whistles and a lot of extra shit, like the giant stone wall surrounding it to protect our family from the vultures also known as the press.

There was one thing, though, our sprawling compound never had. A pool.

The fact my wife found her mother face down in her swimming pool when she was just a child, the pool water pink from all the blood, was certainly more than enough reason that our family home not contain the one thing Rimmel feared.

There was a flaw with that logic, though. One that became apparent the older all the kids became.

Not having a pool—not exposing our children to water and water safety—was partly irresponsible. It was sort of like inviting a terrible accident. My kids, niece, and nephew needed to know how to swim. How to be safe around water.

And hell, having a pool was fun. If you weren't frightened of it, that is.

When spring blossomed here in Maryland, the subject of a pool came up, from the mouth of our five-year-old niece Nova. At first, I rebuffed it (of course, doing so gently) because I wasn't about to put my wife in that kind of position, seeing her uncomfortable in her own home.

I still remembered the way her eyes would skirt to the pool and then away when I lived in the pool house at my parents'. I recalled easily the night she fell in the very same pool and sank like a rock because fear had frozen her limbs.

Everyone in the house understood her reasons for hating the water, and no one ever questioned if we would ever have a pool. It just was what it was.

Ivy promised Nova she'd get a membership at the country club and take her swimming there in the summer.

It should have been the end of the conversation.

Not to Rim.

A few days later, Rim called a family meeting. Frankly, I was slightly offended. Family meetings were my thing to call. But I got over it pretty fucking fast when she stood up in front of our gathered family, looking all cute with her little belly and messy hair.

Rimmel announced she wanted to get a pool. Here. On the compound.

I vetoed that shit instantly. Braeden, Trent, and Drew were about two seconds behind me. Rim had been through enough in life already. This wasn't something that was necessary, and there was no point in making it hard on her.

Rimmel plopped in my lap and changed my mind. All our minds.

"I can't project my fears onto our kids. I won't do it. It's not fair of me to hold them back because of what happened to me."

"We can take them to the club." I argued.

"Where the press can find us? Where people in town can gossip about us? Where we have to pack the car and drive across town, with four little ones . . . soon to be five?" Rimmel shook her head adamantly. "I'm exhausted just thinking about it."

"Me, too." Ivy agreed.

"It's safer if they learn how to swim, if they enjoy the water. I don't want them to be like me."

"And what about you, Rim?" I pressed. "What about your feelings?"

"Maybe it's time I learned to conquer my fear."

Damn if she didn't impress me. This woman knocked my socks off again and again. She was utterly remarkable and selfless.

"I don't know." Trent spoke up. "It's easy to say . . . but looking at that pool every day is something else."

I nodded in agreement.

"I was thinking we could just put it farther away from the house," Rim replied. "Maybe more toward Trent and Drew's. That way it won't be so close, but it will be close enough to walk the kids down to it."

"We could use that large field across from your house!" Ivy said, glancing at Trent and Drew.

Rimmel nodded. "And put a fence around it. With a gate. And a lock. And a safety cover."

Oh, if we got a pool, that thing would have every safety feature imaginable.

"With five kids running around, it would definitely get some use." Ivy agreed.

I hesitated, not wanting to do anything that could potentially hurt Rimmel. Her small hand caressed my cheek, and I glanced up.

"I think it would fine." She encouraged.

Just then, Blue raced into the room, followed closely by Jax. The two boys were inseparable, barely ever apart.

"Mommy!" he yelled and launched at Rimmel. I reached out and caught him just before he dove onto her belly.

"Whoa there, dude. You trying to crush Mommy?"

Blue laughed, and Rimmel tugged him into her lap.

I groaned. "You guys are heavy!" I tossed my head back against the cushions and pretended to pass out.

"You're silly, Daddy!" Blue laughed.

"What do you think, little Blue-Jay," Rimmel said, tickling his stomach. "Do you think we should get a pool for you to swim in?"

Jax gasped from his place on Drew's lap. "I want to 'wim!" he yelled.

Blue nodded sagely, his blue eyes wide.

"Tell Daddy," she whispered in his ear.

"Pwease, Daddy?" Blue asked. His blond hair had some curl to it and always looked like he stuck his finger in a light socket.

I leaned forward and glanced at my brothers. A silent conversation passed between the four of us.

"Geez," Ivy muttered. "There they go again, Rim. Acting like we don't live here."

"But we love you, baby," B told her.

I sighed. "I'll call a couple places and get some bids."

Rimmel's face lit up, and she smiled at Blue.

"Go tell your sister we're getting a pool," Drew told Jax.

Jax jumped down and ran around the couch. "Come on, Jay!" he yelled as he disappeared.

Seconds later, Blue was off Rim's lap and running off calling Nova's name.

And now here we were, months later, with a pool installed at the compound. It was done earlier than expected, and the kids were already begging B to take them in.

"We can put them off," I told Rim as I drove slowly over the road that led to our house. "Tell them it's not ready to swim in yet."

I was worried the idea of a pool was something a lot easier to swallow for Rim than actually seeing it in the ground. Since they broke ground on it, she'd only been down there once when they were digging.

Rimmel smiled. "Are you kidding? The boys will beg us until their faces turn blue if we don't let them at least go see it."

I stopped the Cat right there in the middle of the road and turned to her.

"My main concern is you, baby. Our kids can swim in the pool when you're ready for it and not a moment sooner."

A soft smile transformed her face and made my dick go hard in my jeans. "I'm okay. Honestly. I want our kids to have this. I don't want to hold them back."

I leaned across the car and claimed her mouth. Her tongue stroked into mine, and I groaned.

"I can't wait 'til tonight," I murmured when I finally pulled away. "I need you."

"Maybe we can get the kids into bed early tonight." Her eyes sparkled.

I groaned. "Hells yeah."

"C'mon, then." She urged. "Let's go. I want to see this pool."

I met her eyes, held them. "If it upsets you at all, brings back memories you don't want, say the word. I want you to be happy."

"I am happy, Romeo. So happy. A pool in our backyard isn't going to change that."

I took her hand and put it over the stick shift in the center of the car, then wrapped mine over hers to shift gears and begin driving again.

"About the pool . . ." I said and tossed her my most charming smile.

She groaned. "What did you do Romeo?"

"I just want you to keep in mind that I wanted it to be beautiful as well as safe. You know, maybe to make it a better experience for you."

Rimmel made another sound and put her free hand on the baby girl inside her. "You hear that, London? That's your daddy's way of telling Mommy he spent way, way too much money."

My heart melted, and I swallowed forcibly past the emotion lumped in my throat.

When I didn't say anything, she glanced up. "What is it?"

"That was the first time I ever heard you call our daughter by her name."

Her eyes softened. "A baby girl."

I picked her hand up off the shifter and kissed the back of it, then cleared my throat. "My girls."

When I said I was wrapped around this baby's finger, I wasn't kidding. The pull I felt to that baby girl was incredible. I loved both my sons . . . more than myself, and I would never say it out loud, but there was something about a baby girl. London. I felt her already. She was a clone of her mother, and that in itself slayed me.

Rimmel burst out laughing, interrupting the marshmallow moment going on inside me. "Look!" she exclaimed and laughed again.

I glanced up and grinned.

All three boys and Nova were in the driveway, wearing bathing suits. Asher had on a pair of goggles.

"Oh my goodness, look how adorable they are!" she cried.

"You'd think they were excited or something," I quipped.

They saw the Hellcat and began jumping up and down, waiving their hands at us. Ivy and B were standing there laughing.

I didn't pull the Cat all the way into the driveway, you know, since there was a parade of monsters in bathing suits. Instead, I parked her where the road opened up in front of the garages.

"Stay," I told Rim and jogged around to get the door for her.

She listened (for once), and I leaned in around her to undo the seatbelt. On my way back, I caressed her belly.

"Mommy! Mommy!" Blue and Asher were yelling as they ran across the pavement to us.

Rimmel laughed and held out her arms.

It wasn't her they ran to, though, but me. They launched themselves like human missiles.

"Whoa!" I exclaimed and caught one, then the other. It was a good thing I played football, because if I didn't, these little rug rats would wear me the hell out.

"You're home!" Blue yelled in my ear.

"I can see you were waiting." I chuckled.

"The pool is ready, Mommy!" he told Rim.

Asher held his arms out to her, and she lifted him off me.

"You shouldn't be lifting that much weight," I fussed.

Rimmel gave me a look that dared me to tell her not to pick up her son again.

"'Wim! 'Wim!" he told her. Rim laughed lightly as her eyes roamed over our youngest son. She wasn't lying when she said they looked just like me. Both of them were little heartbreakers in the making. Asher was mischievous and curious. It was like he came out knowing his big brothers and sisters would protect him, and that gave him an instant streak of bravery. Blue was more serious, but his charm matched mine. My mother melted every single time he called her grandma.

"You ready to see the pool?" Rim asked Ash, running her hand over the short blond hair still growing in. "You already have your goggles on!" She laughed.

He pointed to the obnoxiously large blue goggles on his face. "Uncle Trent gave 'em to me."

"He gave us all some," Blue said, still climbing up my back.

"We tried to keep them contained!" Ivy said, rushing forward. "But the second they saw the equipment trucks leaving, it's like they knew they could swim."

"The water is probably still cold," Rimmel sang.

"We're big boys!" Jax told her, his thick, dark hair ruffling in the summer breeze. "We like it!"

B cackled.

"You're not as big as me!" Nova told them all. She was standing beside Ivy, holding an umbrella over her head.

She was dressed in a one-piece suit covered in ruffles. It was navy blue with metallic gold polka dots all over it. Her hair was dark, just like Braeden's, and hung down to her shoulders. Her eyes were blue like Ivy's.

She was my first experience with a baby. My first niece. And in the fall, she was already starting kindergarten.

"Well, how was the appointment?" Ivy asked, her eyes going down to Rim's stomach.

"It's a girl," she said, like holding in the news was just too hard.

Ivy gasped and ran forward to hug both Rim and Asher. "I'm so excited!" she squealed. "It's about time we get some more girls around here."

"Yeah!" Nova celebrated.

"Aww, you're in for it now, Rome," B told me.

I resisted the urge to give him the finger. Didn't want to show our kids a bad example.

When Ivy moved back, B went toward Rim. Before hugging her, though, he lifted Asher out of her arms and held him up the air, making him giggle. "Uncle B!" he yelled.

"Love ya, kid," he said and set him down. "But it's my turn to hug your mommy."

B swooped in and wrapped his arms around Rim, lifting her off her feet and spinning her in a circle.

"Be careful!" I growled. What the hell was he thinking?

B slowed, then set her on her feet but hugged her still. His eyes met mine over her shoulder, and I saw the amused glint in their depths. "You think I'm bad with a baby girl . . . just wait. Rome's gonna be ten times worse."

This time I didn't hold back. I gave him the finger.

"Rome!" B gasped like he was offended—what the fuck ever—and pulled away from my wife. Finally.

"You were asking for it and you know it," Ivy said, smacking him in the chest. B grabbed Ivy, dipped her in the driveway, and planted a loud kiss on her.

"Ew!" Nova yelled. Blue and Jax echoed her instantly.

Rim's eyes found mine, and we shared a moment of solitude in the middle of our chaotic family.

I love you so fucking much, my eyes told her.

So fucking much, she answered.

She held her hand out to Ash and then Blue. He practically jumped off my back to rush to her side. "Come on," she said, moving in front of me. "Let's go see the pool Daddy spent too much money on."

"How much money?" Jax asked.

"Thirty dollars!" Nova told him.

I hung back and watched them go, my wife and my two sons, my entire life.

B sidled up to me and watched Ivy go with their two kids. His fist stretched out between us. "Congrats on the daughter, bro."

I pounded it out. "Thanks, man."

"I don't know how we did it, Rome, but we have more than I ever thought possible."

I grunted. "I know."

"It's a good life," he said.

I slapped him on the back. "A damn good life."

Made in the USA
Middletown, DE
14 October 2017